Comes a Pale Rider

Comes a Pale Rider

Caitlín R. Kiernan

Subterranean Press ✧ 2020

First Edition

ISBN
978-1-59606-985-5

Subterranean Press
PO Box 190106
Burton, MI 48519

subterraneanpress.com
www.caitlinrkiernan.com
greygirlbeast.livejournal.com
Twitter: @auntbeast

Manufactured in the United States of America

In memory of Joanne Ramey Cage (1934–2019)

The heart has vision that defeats the dark
of nothingness, and puts nonbeing to flight.
The dark is but a shadow of the light. ~ J.R.C.

And I looked, and behold: a pale horse
And his name that sat on him was death,
And Hell followed with him.
~ Johnny Cash

Somebody left the door open and
the wrong dogs came home.
~ The Nameless Stranger

Well, the night is dark
And the night is deep
And its jaws are open wide.
~ Nick Cave and the Bad Seeds

Table of Contents

Bus Fare

She knows there was a town here once, because the deserted streets are lined with deserted, boarded-up buildings. The roofs of some have sagged and collapsed in on themselves, and one has burned almost to the ground. And if there were once a town here, there must have been people, too. So, she thinks, maybe only their ghosts live here now. She's seen plenty of ghosts, and they usually prefer places living people have forsaken. These are the things the albino girl named Dancy Flammarion is thinking, these things and a few more, while the black-haired, olive-skinned girl talks. The girl is sitting on the wooden bench with Dancy. Her clothes are threadbare and she isn't wearing any shoes. She might be fourteen, and she could pass for Dancy's shadow. Dancy glances from her duffel bag to the faded bus sign, but she doesn't look into the girl's eyes. She doesn't like what she's seen there.

"Are you sure the bus still stops here?" she asks, interrupting the girl, who said her name was Maisie. Maybe, Dancy thinks, people named Maisie look different in South Carolina than they do in Florida and Georgia, because the girl doesn't look much like a Maisie.

"Last anyone bothered telling me," the girl replies. She doesn't have any luggage, not even a duffel bag, and Dancy is pretty sure she isn't waiting on a bus that may or may not come. "I still don't understand why you gave up a perfectly good ride and decided to Hound it instead."

"Hound it?" Dancy asks, and the girl who might be named Maisie jabs a thumb at the faded Greyhound sign. The thumbnail, like all her other fingernails, is thick and chocolate colored.

"The sun was setting," she says. "That's why I didn't stay in the car. The dead boy and girl in the trunk were waking up, and the Bailiff said they'd be hungry, and how it would be best if I walked a while."

"The Bailiff," Maisie says and smiles. "Yeah, I heard of him. Man ain't got no right name, you know." And then she stares silently at Dancy for a while. Dancy watches the empty streets of the empty town. She sees a huge black dog cross the street.

"You sure seem to know an awful lot of things," Dancy says to the girl.

"That I do," Maisie admits. "That I do. You're getting a reputation, Dancy."

That's what the monster in Waycross told her, and the crazy women in the big house in Savannah, and the Bailiff, he seemed to know, too.

"You're kinda like Joan of Arc, right?" the girl asks.

"No," Dancy tells her. "I'm not like Joan of Arc."

"How's that?" Maisie wants to know. "You got yourself an angel who tells you where to find the monsters, and then you kill them. You're just a crazy girl doing the righteous work of the Lord. Sounds like Joan of Arc to me."

"I'm not like Joan of Arc," Dancy says again. "And I'm not crazy."

"Have it your way," Maisie sighs and lights a cigarette. She offers one to Dancy, but Dancy's never smoked a cigarette in her life, and she doesn't mean to start tonight. "How old are you, anyway? Fifteen?"

"Sixteen," Dancy tells her. "Seventeen soon now."

"You ain't got not folks?"

"Not anymore."

Of course, Dancy suspects Maisie already knows the answers to all the questions she's asking, and this is just going through the motions. She knew about Bainbridge, and the old man with the caged panther, the cat who was really a woman, and Maisie knew about the Bailiff and the vampire children, the monster in Waycross who wore other people's skin because it didn't have one of its own. She knew about the nine women in Savannah who were cannibals and dug up corpses and…did other things she'd rather not wonder about. She knew how many of them Dancy's killed. So, she knows all that, surely she knows how old Dancy is, and that her mother and grandmother are both dead.

Dancy sits back down on the wooden bench near the Greyhound sign, trying not to dwell on how thirsty she is, or whether or not a bus will ever show up, or what it means that the girl calling herself Maisie knows so much. The night is almost as hot as the day was, though at least there's no sun. No sun, so she doesn't need the raggedy black umbrella leaning against the bench. The air smells like cooling asphalt, kudzu, and pine trees. And it also smells like dog, which is the way that Maisie smells.

"Why do you smell like dog?" Dancy asks, gazing at the street, trying to catch another glimpse of the big black mutt she spotted a few minutes before.

"That's not a very polite thing to ask a stranger," Maisie says, pretending to be offended.

"The way you keep asking *me* questions, didn't think you'd much mind. You ask a lot of questions."

"And you don't smell so sweet your own self, Dancy Flammarion."

It rained a few days ago, and that's the closest Dancy's come to a bath since the night she stripped down and bathed in a muddy stream. And that bath, it was before the Bailiff and the dead children found her hitchhiking along Route 76, but she's having trouble recalling exactly how many days have passed since then.

"It's just sweat," Dancy says. "Just dirt and sweat. I don't smell like a dog." There's an old Coke machine outside an abandoned gas station across the road, and she wishes the gas station weren't abandoned and she had change for a cold drink.

Maisie sighs, very loudly, and she asks, "So, you just wanna cut to the chase, then? Stop dancing round the truth of the matter?"

"You ask a lot of questions," Dancy tells the girl for the second time. And finally, she makes herself turn and look directly at the dark-haired girl. In the moonlight, the girl's eyes glint iridescent red, like the eyeshine of alligators and possums.

"The night's young," the girl tells her. "And I like some sport before dinner. Didn't think you'd mind all that much. Didn't think you'd care one way or the other." The girl who says her name is Maisie smiles and shows off a lot more teeth than she ought to have. Maisie takes a last draw off her cigarette and flicks it away.

"I ain't scared of you," Dancy says, trying hard to sound like she means it. She looks at the duffel bag, but tries not to *look* like she's looking. The handle of the big carving knife is sticking out of the bag. Maisie, she's one of the ones the seraph didn't bother to tell her was coming. That happens sometimes.

"Hardly thought you would be, not after all you done and seen, little Miss Joan of Arc cutting a swath across the countryside, laying all the bad folk low. Figure you ain't smart enough to be scared of nothing."

"Someone sent you?" Dancy wants to know. "The women in Savannah, did they send you after me?"

"No one *sent* me. We got curious, when we heard you'd be passing our way. Then this bitch made a bet. I drew the short straw, that's all."

"Sometimes I don't know they're coming." Dancy says it out loud, though she hadn't meant to, had only meant to think those words to herself.

"Well, that makes it a tiny bit more fair, don't you think, not getting the drop on people."

"You ain't people. I don't kill people."

"Strictly speaking, Snow White, that's not exactly factual. Not Gospel truth, I mean."

Dancy gives up on the duffel bag, because there's no way she'd ever have time to reach it and get hold of the knife before the olive-skinned girl who smells like a dog will be on her. She turns back to Maisie.

"You ain't the first ever called me that, you know. Snow White, I mean."

"I expect not. That mop of cornsilk hair, those pink rabbity eyes, that skin like you been playing in the flour bin. Figure you hear it a lot."

"Ain't never met one quite like you before," Dancy says, which isn't true, but she's stalling for time. If she has another minute or two, maybe she can think of a way to reach her knife or some other way to stop Maisie from eating her. "I never really believed in werewolves. Didn't know they were real."

Maisie furrows her brow and leans a little nearer Dancy. Her breath stinks of raw meat. "You're kidding me. You hitch rides with vampires, but you don't believe in werewolves?"

"Oh, now I do," Dancy says. "Sure. Just not before."

A warm wind stirs the underbrush at the edge of the road and the beard of Spanish moss in a nearby stand of live oaks. Dancy smells herself sweating – fresh sweat, not stale – and Maisie wrinkles her nose and flares her wide nostrils (which didn't seem quite so wide only a few seconds before).

"Oh, I almost forgot," Maisie says, and she produces something from…well, Dancy isn't sure where she was hiding it, but now there's an old cardboard cigar box in the girl's hand.

"That's mine," Dancy tells her. "I lost it –"

"– when you murdered them poor folks down in Waycross."

"Weren't folks, neither of them."

"Kinda depends on your point of view," says the olive-skinned girl who claims her name is Maisie.

"Well, it's mine. So you should give it back."

"I should?" the girl asks, and looks inside. "Mostly just a bunch of junk," she says.

And maybe it looks that way to her, or to anyone who isn't Dancy. But junk gets precious when junk's all you've got left, and in her head Dancy counts off the contents of the cigar box, all that's left of her life *before* all that was left to her was the road and her knife, the seraph and the parade of horrors it expects her to kill. She glances over her shoulder, and she's not at all surprised to find the angel looming behind the bench, looking over her and Maisie. The seraph's tattered muslin and silk robes are even blacker than the night, than the dark inside the deserted shop fronts. They flutter and flap in a fierce and holy wind that touches nothing else. The angel's four ebony wings are spread wide, and it holds a burning sword high above its four shimmering kaleidoscope faces, both skeletal hands gripped tightly around the weapon's silver hilt. It stares down at her, and makes a sound like thunder that surely isn't thunder.

Just this once, she thinks, while Maisie paws through the cigar box. *Just this once, you could do the deed your own self. Seems like I earned that much.*

The angel doesn't answer her, but Dancy knows its moods well enough to know it's not about to intercede. Those aren't the rules, and it never breaks the rules. She looks at Maisie again, who's taking stuff out of the box and lining it up on the bench between them. So far, there are two plastic checkers (one black, one red), a tiny, battered copy of the New Testament that had been her mother's, and her grandmother's rosary, a spent shotgun shell she found at the edge of the road, two buttons, a green crayon, and a little statue of the Virgin Mary.

"It's mine, and you should give it back," she says to Maisie.

"You know better. Ain't nothing ever that easy." Maisie takes out a Patsy Cline cassette and a rubber band, then lines them up with all the rest.

"Maybe I could win it back," Dancy suggests, not taking her eyes off all the meager treasures she'd never hoped to see again. "Maybe we could have some sort of contest, and if I win, you gotta give it back."

Maisie looks up from the box. Her red eyes glimmer, and Dancy sees that her eyebrows meet in the middle, though they hadn't before. Maisie is holding a matchbox between those dark nails that have become claws. Inside the matchbox is thirty-five cents in pennies, dimes, and nickels that Dancy found along the highways.

"What do you have in mind? And what's in it for me? I had in mind I'd just eat you and be done with it. Why go complicating the situation?"

"Thought you wanted some sport."

Maisie stares at her, and Dancy wonders how her eyes can have eyeshine, when there's no light shining on them. *There's the moon,* she thinks, then pushes the thought away.

"What you got in mind," the girl asks her.

"You any good at riddles?"

The girl, who is very slowly becoming not so much a girl, but something else, replies, "Not too shabby. Is that what you propose, a riddle game?"

"Yeah, and if I win, I get my box back, and you let me go. You win, I won't put up a struggle."

The girl thing scratches at her chin and seems to consider the offer. "Just three riddles," she says, "so there can't be no tie."

"Fine, just three riddles."

"And I go first."

"Fine, you go first."

"But how do I know you ain't gonna up and renege if you lose?"

"Everything you heard about me, ever heard of me telling lies?" Dancy asks.

"No, but still and all. I'd like some insurance."

Dancy Flammarion glances at the angel again, and it stares back at her with all its eight eyes. *Maybe you're gonna help after all,* she thinks directly at it. "Yeah, okay," she says to the werewolf. "I swear on the name of my angel I won't go back on my word."

Maisie looks surprised and chews her coal-colored lips. "That's a lot more than I expected. You'll say its name aloud and swear on it? You do that, you can't lie."

"That's what I just said, ain't it?"

Maisie stops taking Dancy's treasures out of the cigar box and nods her head. "Deal," she smiles, flashing all those sharp teeth. Her ears have grown to points, and each one has a small tuft of hair at the tip. Behind Dancy, the seraph makes an awful, ugly noise and beats its wings, but she ignores it. The angel had its chance to help, but it was willing to stand by and let her be eaten and not even raise a finger, after all she's done just because it told her to.

"I get two riddles," Maisie says. "You just get the one," which hardly seems fair. The game's rigged in the werewolf's favor.

Dancy almost doesn't protest, but then says, "We could have five, instead. Five riddles, and I get two, and you get three. Still, no chance of a tie. Like you said, night's still young."

"Ain't *that* young," the werewolf says, and licks at its lips with a mottled tongue that's too long for a fourteen-year-old girl named Maisie. "You don't like the terms, I can always keep the box and eat you right here and now, get it over with."

"Fine," Dancy sighs. "Three riddles, you first," and then she swears on the name of the seraph. She says its name aloud, which she's never done before. This time, she can tell Maisie also hears the thunder, and a trickle of blood leaks from the werewolf's noise. She wipes it away and grins.

"Well, ain't *that* just God's own fucking magic," she says. "And here I thought all I'd won was a free meal and a notch on the bedpost."

"It ain't magic, and you ain't won nothing yet," Dancy tells her. Then she reaches out and picks up the red checker. Maisie doesn't try to stop her. "Your move," she says to the crimson-eyed girl.

"I don't have to tell you, Dancy Flammarion, you lose this first one, and I get the second one right, that's all she wrote. Won't be need of a third riddle, it goes that way, will there."

"No," Dancy scowls. "You *don't* have to tell me that. Being an albino doesn't make me stupid."

"Just let me think a second."

Dancy shrugs and says, "The night's not *that* young, Maisie." She rubs the checker between her thumb and index finger. She smiles, wishing her smile was half so unnerving as the werewolf's.

"Then you answer me this, Joan of Arc," says Maisie, and she recites:

"Although it never asked a thing

Of any mortal man,

Everybody answers it

As quickly as he can."

Dancy shuts her eyes, because sometimes she thinks better that way. She closes her eyes, though maybe that's not the best thing to do when you're sitting on a bench with a werewolf who wants and fully intends to eat you. She lets the four lines run over and over again in her head.

"You don't know, do you?"

Dancy opens her eyes and sets the checker back down between them. "A knock at a door," she says, and the words come out more triumphantly than she'd meant them to come out. Maisie glowers and stares at the gravel and weeds between her bare feet.

"My turn," Dancy says, and she already knows the riddle she's going to ask. She's known it since she was a little girl:

"Green as grass, but grass it ain't.

White as snow, but snow it ain't.

Red as blood, but blood it ain't.

Black as ink, but ink it ain't."

"Your grammar's atrocious," the werewolf grunts and continues staring at the space between its feet. It repeats the riddle aloud several times. Dancy reaches into the cigar box and takes out her old St. Christopher's medal. The silver's tarnished, but she feels better just holding it, because St. Christopher's the patron saint of travelers, and she's been traveling for what feels like a very long time. It feels like she's been traveling her whole life.

"Don't know, do you," she whispers hopefully.

But Maisie snaps her fingers, her claws snicking together like a pair of scissors. "A blackberry," Maisie says and raises her head. Her hair's a lot longer than it was, shaggy and almost not like hair at all. Almost like a mane. "A ripening blackberry. That's it, right?"

"Yeah," Dancy says, then opens her hand and glares at the medal in her palm. First the angel, now a saint that's supposed to be watching over her, but clearly isn't. *Tonight,* she thinks, *all Heaven's gone and turned its back on me.*

"So, this one, she's the bitch of the litter. She's all do or die. You better stew on it long and hard." And then Maisie says:

"Red in the valley,

Red on the hill.

Feed it, live it will.

Water it, it will die.

This is true, and not a lie."

This time, Dancy doesn't shut her eyes. Maisie's a lot more wolf than girl now, her face become a muzzle, her legs the long, powerful hindquarters of a beast. There's only deeper shades of night waiting in back of Dancy's eyelids, and it's bad enough sitting across from the monster as it is, with only moonlight. The sun's hard on her skin, and she's rarely wished for sunrise. But she wishes for it now, even though it's still hours away.

"How do I know you're gonna keep your promise," she says. "I gave you insurance, but you didn't give me nothing but your word."

"Then my word's all you got, Snow White. You know the answer or don't you?"

"You didn't set a time limit," Dancy replies, then repeats the riddle aloud. "Red in the valley, red on the hill…"

"That's what I said," Maisie says, only she sounds more like she's growling now than talking.

Dancy ignores her. She knows the wolf is a deceitful, wicked demon, that it's only trying to distract her, trip her up, make it harder for her to concentrate. "Feed it," she continues, "live it will. Water it, it will die."

"This is true, and not a lie," the werewolf growls, then makes a noise that Dancy supposes is meant to be a laugh, if wolves could laugh.

A minute more comes and goes. Then five, and ten. Then Maisie (if she still is or ever was a Maisie) growls, "Time's up."

"No," Dancy says. "We didn't set a time limit."

"We didn't *not* set a time limit, and I'm bored and hungry, and I say time's up. You *don't* know the answer, and sitting here all damn night long ain't gonna help you conjure up the right answer." There's finality and a faint hint of exasperation in the creature's gruff voice, and Dancy knows there's absolutely no point trying to reason with it. Maisie never intended to let her live. The riddles were nothing but a game of cat and mouse.

"Yeah," Dancy says, sparing another quick glimpse at the angel. "You win the game." She's pretty sure she's never seen the seraph half so angry before. When she looks back at the werewolf, its gotten up off the bench and is standing on its hind feet. It towers over her, grown at least a yard taller while they traded riddles. The girl's clothes hang in shreds from the lean, ribsy body.

"Looks like you don't get enough to eat," Dancy tells the wolf and points at its ribs.

"Tonight I will," it sneers, and saliva drips from its mouth and spatters on Dancy's duffel bag. "Tonight, I get a feast."

Dancy nods, gripping the St. Christopher's medal as tightly as she can. "What big eyes you have," she says, then flips the medal like it was a quarter, and it strikes the werewolf squarely in its right eye. There's a sizzling sound, and the smell of burning pork. A second later, there's a soft pop when the monster's eye boils and bursts. It howls, a howl that's nothing but pain and anger, and it clutches at its face, trying to brush away the smoldering talisman seared into its flesh.

"Wasn't even halfway sure that was gonna work," Dancy mutters, and she leans over and draws the carving knife from the green canvas bag. The blade shines dully under the moon. "Thought maybe that was just in books."

The werewolf lunges for her then, its steaming jaws open wide as the gates of any hell, its left eye blazing and nothing but a scorched black pit where its right had been. Dancy swings the knife, *her* sword, opening the beast's throat from ear to ear, slicing through jugular and carotid arteries, through muscle and larynx, cutting all the way to the bone. The blade lodges firmly in a vertebra, and as the werewolf stumbles backwards, gurgling, strangling on its own blood, the knife's yanked from Dancy's hand with enough force that she loses her balance and falls hard on her hands and knees.

"It's a fire, puppy," she says, not caring whether or not the beast can hear her. "The answer's a fire."

An hour later, and Dancy's dragged Maisie's naked body into the woods behind the bus stop. Dead, she became nothing but a fourteen-year-old girl again, so she wasn't all that heavy. Dancy covered her decently with magnolia and sycamore leaves and with branches torn from bushes. She figured the coyotes and wild dogs, maybe coons and feral pigs and whatever else sniffed out the corpse, would do the rest. Now, she's back at the bench, wiping the blood from her knife and she holds the cigar box tucked under one arm. All her treasures are safe inside it again, everything but the St. Christopher's

medal, which melted away to nothing. The seraph has gone, took its leave the moment she killed the werewolf that meant to kill her, and Dancy knows it won't ever be back. It said not one word as it departed in a veil of flame and smoke, but there wasn't anything it might have said she didn't already know. It plays by the rules, laws older than the universe, and she's sure there's always someone else willing to do its bidding.

"That's only fair and right," she says, and slips the knife back into the duffel bag. "I was scared. I didn't want to die, not here. Not tonight. So, I went and took your name in vain. I spoke your name, *used* your name, then cheated. I'm not gonna say it ain't fair. I knew better."

But Dancy Flammarion's never been on her own before, and that part frightens her almost as much as Maisie did. On the road alone and no shelter in a storm, and no angelic host to tell her where to go and what to expect when she gets there. She's already done so much damage that every speck of evil, every fiend for hundreds of miles around, knows her name. They whisper it in their hiding places, and make plans for her undoing. And if she needed proof that the hunter has become the hunted, the werewolf was precisely that. She doesn't need to be told twice.

There's a rumble, and for just half a second, there's hope it might be the seraph. That maybe her sin wasn't so unforgivable, after all. But then she sees the headlights of the Greyhound bus moving towards her through the deserted town. Dancy stares up at the night sky for a moment, all the stars, the empty space between the stars, and the moon that must have been the girl's goddess, but couldn't be bothered to save her. Any more than the angel could be bothered to save Dancy. As the bus pulls to a stop, raising clouds of dust and grit, she shoulders her heavy duffel bag and waits for the door to swing open.

BUS FARE

I would say that everything that needs saying about this story is covered in the afterword (which, hopefully, you didn't read first), except… I would add that Dancy's riddle was one my maternal grandfather, Gordy Monroe Ramey (1911–1977), used to tell us when I was a kid. He had this way of running the last bit together into only two words, so that "But ink it ain't" became "But inkydaink." Also, Dancy's cigar box of treasures actually exists and now may be found in the Caitlín R. Kiernan Papers at the John Hay Library (Brown University).

Dancy vs. the Pterosaur

Dancy Flammarion sits out the storm in the ruins of a Western Railway of Alabama boxcar, hauled years and years ago off rusting steel rails and summarily left for dead. Left for kudzu vines and possums, copperheads and wandering albino girls looking for shelter against sudden summer rains, shelter from thunder and lightning and wind. It's sweltering inside the boxcar, despite the downpour, and, indeed, she imagines it might be hotter now than before the rain began. That happens sometimes, in the long Dog Day South Alabama broil. The floor of the boxcar is covered in dead kudzu leaves and rotting plywood, except a few places where she can see the metal floor rusted straight through. The rain against the roof sizzles loudly, singing like frying meat; she sits with her back to one wall, gazing out the open sliding doors at the sheeting rain.

Dancy fishes a can of Libby's Vienna sausages from her duffel bag, a few mouthfuls of protein shoplifted from a Winn-Dixie on the outskirts of Enterprise, three days back the way she's come. She pops the lid and drinks the salty, oily juice before digging the pasty little sausages out with her fingers. Dancy hates Vienna sausages, but beggars can't be choosers, that's what her grandmother always said. *Neither can thieves,* she thinks. *Thieves can't be choosers, either.*

When she's done, she uses a few paper napkins – also lifted from the Winn-Dixie – to wipe her fingers as clean as she can get them. She catches a little rainwater in the empty can. It's warm and tastes like grease, but it helps her thirst a little. Starving has never scared her as much as the possibility of dying of thirst, and she's drunk from worse than an empty Vienna sausage can.

She closes her eyes and manages half an hour's sleep, a half hour at most. But she dreams of another life she might have lived. She dreams of a talking blackbird – a red-winged blackbird – and the ghost of a girl who was a werewolf before she died. Before Dancy had to kill her. It isn't a good dream. When she wakes up, the rain has stopped, the clouds have gone, and the world outside the boxcar is wet and steaming in the brilliant August sun. It can't be very long past noon. She pisses through one of the holes in the floor of the boxcar, already thirsty and wishing she had a few more cans full of the oily sausage-flavored rainwater. She gathers up her green Army surplus duffel bag, worn and patched, patches sewn over patches, and she finds her sunglasses. She stole those, too, from a convenience store somewhere down in Florida. The seraph has never said anything about her thefts. Necessary evils and all, tiny transgressions in the service of the greater good. And she's made it a rule never to take anything worth more than ten dollars. She keeps a tally, written in pencil on the back of a tourism pamphlet advertising Tarpon Springs. As of today, she owes seventy-three dollars and fifteen cents. She knows she'll never pay any of it back, but she keeps the tally, anyway.

Dancy climbs down out of the boxcar and opens the black umbrella, almost as patched as the duffel bag; two of the spokes poke out through the nylon fabric.

"Where am I going this time?" she asks, but no one and nothing answers. It's been days now since the angel appeared, all wrath and fire and terrible swift swords. She's on her own, until it shows up and shoves her this way or that way. So, she wandered north to Enterprise, then east to this abandoned and left for dead boxcar not far from the banks of the muddy Choctawhatchee River. She makes her way back to the road, rural route something or something else, another anonymous county highway. She parts waist-high goldenrod and stinging nettles like Moses dividing the Red Sea. Her T-shirt, jeans, and boots are close to soaked through by the time she reaches the road, which makes her wonder why she bothered taking shelter in the boxcar.

The road is wet and dark and shiny as cottonmouth scales.

Without direction, without instruction, left to her own devices, there's nothing to do but walk, and so she resumes the march eastward, towards Georgia, still a good thirty or forty miles away. But that's just as a crow flies, not as she has to walk down this road. And there's no particular reason to aim for Georgia, except she has no idea where else she'd go.

Dancy walks and sings to herself to take her mind off the heat.

"I'm just a poor wayfaring stranger.

I'm traveling through this world of woe.

Yet there's no sickness, no toil nor danger

In that bright land to which I go.

I'm going home to see my mother…"

She's walked no more than half a mile when she sees the dragon.

At first, she thinks she's seeing nothing but a very large turkey vulture, soaring on the thermals rising up off the blacktop. But then it wheels nearer, far up and silhouetted black against the blue, blue sky, and she can see that whatever it is, it isn't a turkey vulture. She doesn't think it's even a bird, because, for one thing, it doesn't seem to have feathers. For another, it's *huge*. She's seen big pelicans, but they were, at most, only half as big as the thing in the sky, wing tip to wing tip. She's seen egrets and herons and eagles, but nothing like this. She stands in the middle of the road and watches, transfixed, not thinking, yet, that maybe this is something to be afraid of, something that could do her harm.

It's a dragon, she thinks. *I'm seeing a dragon, and the angel didn't warn me.*

I didn't even know dragons were real.

The thing in the sky screams. Or it sounds like a scream to Dancy, and the cry sends chill bumps up and down her arms, makes the hairs at the base of her neck stand on end. It's almost directly overhead now, the creature. She shields her eyes, trying to shut out the glare of the sun, hoping for a better view. It's sort of like a giant bat, the dragon, because its wings look leathery, taut membranes stretched between bony struts, and the creature *might* be covered with short, velvety hair like a bat's. But it's hard to be *sure* about these details, it's so far overhead. The strangest part of all is the dragon's head. There's a crest on the back of its narrow skull, a crest almost as long as its beak, and the crest makes its head look sort of like a boomerang.

The dragon flaps its enormous wings, seven yards across if they're an inch, and screams again. And that's when Dancy hears a voice somewhere to her left, calling out from the thicket of beech and pine and creeper vines at the edge of the road. For just a second, she thinks maybe it's her angel, come, belatedly, to warn her about the dragon and to tell her what she's supposed to do. Come to reveal this wrinkle in its grand skein – its holy plan for her, whatever comes next. But *this* isn't the angel at all. It's only the voice of a girl who sounds impatient and, maybe, a little frightened.

"Get outta the road," the girl tells her, somehow managing to whisper and raise her voice at the same time, cautiously raising her voice only as much as she dares. "It's gonna *see* you if you don't get outta the middle of the damn road."

"Maybe it's supposed to see me," Dancy says aloud, though she'd only meant to think that to herself. Already she's reaching for the Bowie knife tucked into the waistband of her jeans.

"Get outta the *road*," the girl shouts, actually *shouting* this time, no longer trying not to be heard by the hairy black thing in the sky.

Dancy draws her knife, and the sun flashes off the stainless steel blade. Her hand is sweaty around the handle, that stout hilt carved from the antler of a white-tailed buck.

The dragon soars and banks, and then it dives for her.

Why wasn't I warned? Why didn't you tell me there are dragons?

But then she's being pulled, hauled along with enough force and urgency that she almost loses her balance to tumble head over heels off the asphalt and into a tangle of blackberry briars.

"Jesus," the girl says, "are you *simple?* Are you *crazy?*"

Dancy looks back over her shoulder just in time to see the dragon swoop low above the road; there can be no doubt that it was coming for her.

"You saw that?" she asks, and the girl tugging her deeper into the woods replies, "Yeah, I saw it. Of course I saw it. What were you *doing* back there? What did you *think* you were doing?"

And it's not that Dancy doesn't have an answer for her, it's just that there's something in the scolding, exasperated tone of the girl's voice that makes her feel foolish, so she doesn't reply.

"What the Sam Hill were you doing out there anyway, strolling down the road with a knapsack and a knife? You a hitchhiker or some sort of hobo?"

I'm going home to see my mother.
I'm going home no more to roam.
I'm just a-going over Jordan,
I'm just a-going over home.

The girl has stopped dragging Dancy, but she hasn't released the death grip on her wrist and is still leading her through the woods. The girl's short hair is braided close to her scalp in neat cornrows, and her skin, thinks Dancy, is almost the same deep brown as a Hershey bar.

Beads of sweat stand out on the girl's forehead and upper lip; a bead of sweat hangs from the tip of her nose.

"I ain't no hobo," Dancy says. "I don't hitchhike, either. And it's not a knapsack, it's a duffel bag. It was my great-grandfather's duffel bag, when he fought in World War I. He fought the Germans in the Argonne Forest in 1918, and this was his duffel bag."

They've come to a small clearing near a stream, a place where the trees and vines have left enough room for the sun to reach the ground. Dancy asks the girl to please let go of her, and the girl does. Once again, Dancy looks back towards the road and the dragon. There's a mounting sense that all of this is wrong, that she hasn't done what she was *meant* to do back there. She doesn't run from the monsters; she doesn't ever run.

The air here is hot and still. It smells like pine sap and cicadas. The air here smells *hot,* and Dancy imagines that, rain or no rain, one careless match would be enough to set the world on fire. She drops her heavy duffel bag onto the ground, slips the knife back into her waistband, and looks about her.

"Who are you, anyway?" she asks the girl.

"Who are you?"

"I asked first," Dancy replies.

The girl who dragged her into the forest, away from the boomerang-headed dragon, shrugs, and alright, she says, whatever. "My name's Jezzie, Jezzie Lilligraven."

"Jessie?"

"No, *Jezzie,*" says the girl. "With z's. It's short for Jezebel."

Dancy turns her attention back to the clearing. There's a big wooden packing crate near the center, and a door and window has been cut into the side facing her. The wood is emblazoned with MAYTAG, and THIS END UP, and a red arrow pointing heavenward. There's a piece of pale blue calico cloth tacked over the window and there's a door made from corrugated tin. There aren't any hinges; it's just propped in place.

"That's sort of an odd name," Dancy says, glancing up at the sky, because the dragon might have followed them. "Who'd name their daughter after Jezebel. She was an evil woman who worshipped Baal and persecuted the prophets of God and his people. She was thrown from a window and fed to wild dogs by Jehu for her sins. Who would name their daughter after someone like that?"

The girl stares at Dancy a moment, rolls her eyes, then heads for the wooden packing crate.

"Yeah, so what's *your* name, Little Miss Sunshine, and, by the way, you're very welcome."

"Dancy. My name is Dancy Flammarion. And very welcome for what?"

The girl lifts the corrugated tin and sets it aside, leaning it against the outer wall of the crate. Dancy thinks it looks cool in there, within the arms of those shadows.

"Dancy Flammarion? *That's* your name?"

"Yeah. So?"

The girl shakes her head and steps into the packing crate, vanishing from view. Dancy can still hear her, though.

"Just, with a name like that, I wouldn't be ragging on anyone else's. Ever heard of throwing rocks in glass houses?"

"It's a town up in Pickens County," Dancy says. "My grandmother was born in Dancy, so my mother named me Dancy."

"You gonna stand out there or what?" the girl says from inside the packing crate.

"Well, you haven't invited me in."

There's a pause, and then, with an exaggerated politeness, the girl says, "Dancy Flammarion, would you like to come inside?"

"Yeah," Dancy says, checking the sky one last time.

It isn't as cool inside the crate as she'd hoped, but it's cooler than it had been inside the abandoned Western Railway of Alabama boxcar. There's a threadbare rug covering the floor, a rug the color of green apples; there's a cot set up at one end of the crate and a folding aluminum card table at the other. There's a blue blanket at the foot of the bed, neatly folded, and a pillow. Books are stacked under the cot and along the walls. On the table, there's a box of graham crackers and another box of chocolate Moon Pies. There are also two cans of pork and beans. Beneath the table is a styrofoam cooler and a plastic jug of water.

"You live here?" Dancy asks, eyeing the water jug, aware now just how parched her mouth and throat is.

"No," the girl replies. "*I'm* not a hobo. I stay down on Parish Road, close to Fort Rucker. That's an Army base."

"I'm *not* a hobo. I done told you that already."

"Says you. You're the one out hitchhiking with a knapsack."

Dancy frowns and looks around the crate again.

"All these books yours?"

"Yeah," the girl says. "They were my granddad's, and now they're mine. My daddy was gonna throw 'em all out, but I saved them. You can have a seat on the cot there, if your britches ain't too wet and if they ain't muddy."

Dancy pats the butt of her jeans, decides they probably *are* too damp to be sitting on anyone's bed, and so she settles for a place on the rug, instead.

"It's nice in here," Dancy says.

"Thank you," says Jezzie Lilligraven. "This is where I come to be alone and think, to get away from my brothers and just be by myself."

"Well, it's nice," Dancy says again. Then she notices something else on the floor, something else spaced out here and there along the walls of the packing crate, between the stacks of books – there are pint Mason jars and big two and three quart jars that might once have held dill pickles or pickled eggs or pickled pig's feet, but now they're filled with clear liquid and dead things. Dancy looks at Jezzie and then back at the jars. The one nearest Dancy has a big king snake, black coils and links of cream-colored scales, and the one next to it holds a baby alligator.

"That's my herpetology collection," Jezzie says, before Dancy has a chance to ask, and then the girl picks up a yellow and pink waffle-weave dishrag and wipes the sweat off her face.

Dancy looks up at her. "Your what?" she asks.

"It's the study of reptiles and amphibians. *Herpetology.*"

"You keep dead things in jars?"

"So I can study them. I caught them myself, and I used rubbing alcohol to preserve them. It ain't so good as formalin, but where am I gonna get that?"

Dancy rubs at her eyes, which feel at least as dry as her throat.

"You want something to drink?" Jezzie asks, like maybe the girl can read her mind. "I got water, and I got water. But it's good sweet water, right from our well."

"Yes, please," Dancy replies, and Jezzie opens the plastic jug and fills a jelly glass halfway full.

"Now, don't drink it too fast," she says. "You'll get cramps. You might throw up, if you drink it too fast."

You think I don't know not to gulp water when I'm this hot and thirsty? she wants to say. *You think I don't know no better?* But she keeps the thoughts to herself and sips the water in the jelly glass.

"I like to think one day I'm gonna go away to college," Jezzie tells her. "I won't, cause we don't have the money, and my grades ain't good enough for no scholarship. But I like to think it, anyway. I have my granddad's books – like you've got your great-granddad's knapsack – and I teach myself everything I can. I don't have to be ignorant, just cause my family can't afford college. I might just wind up working at the Wal-Mart or my auntie's BBQ place, but I don't have to be ignorant."

"Keeping dead snakes in jars, you think that makes you smart?" Dancy asks, and she leans a little nearer the jar with the king snake.

Its eyes are a milky white. She sets her glass down, picks up one of the books, and she reads the cover aloud – *Prehistoric Life* by Percy E. Raymond, Third Printing, Harvard University Press.

See? Dancy thinks. *I ain't ignorant, neither. I can read.*

"That's one of my favorites, that one is," Jezzie tells her. "It's kinda outta date, cause it was published in 1950, and we know lots more now. I mean, scientists know lots more. But it's still one of my favorites. It taught me about evolution and geologic time. My teacher wouldn't teach that, skipped over that part of the textbook so parents wouldn't complain about –"

"Evolution?" Dancy asks, flipping through the yellowing pages. There are photographs of fossils and dinosaurs and skeletons. "You believe in that, in evolution?"

Jezzie is silent a moment. She sits down on the floor by the table.

"Yeah," she says. "Yeah, I do. It's science. It's how everything alive –"

"It's against the Bible," Dancy interrupts, setting the book back down. "The Book of Genesis tells how the world was made."

"In six days," Jezzie says.

"Yes, in six days. And if *that* book says any different it's against God and Jesus, and it's blasphemous."

Jezzie is frowning and looking at her hands. "You sound like my Daddy and Mama and the parson down at First Testament Baptist. You ever *read* a book like that? You ever read about Charles Darwin and natural selection? You heard about Mendel and genetics?"

Dancy puts the book down and picks up her glass again. She takes another swallow, wishing the water were at least a little bit cooler. "No," she says. "I *ain't* never heard of mandolin cosmetics, and I don't read books that go against God."

Jezzie rolls her eyes, and, then, pronouncing each syllable with great care as if she's speaking to someone hard of hearing, she says – "No, *Mendel and genetics.*"

"Not that neither," Dancy tells her.

"What *you've* got is a closed mind, Dancy Flammarion. You think you know what's what, and so you won't let nothin' else in."

"I know I didn't come from no dirty ol' monkey," Dancy mutters.

"Oh, but it don't bother you to think you came from a fistful of mud?"

Outside, the cicadas have begun singing, and it sounds to Dancy like the trees are in pain, the bugs giving voice to the aching of bark and loblolly pine needles.

Jezzie says, "And you probably think the whole wide world is only ten thousand years old. I *bet* that's what you think."

"No, I don't *know* how old the world is, *Jezebel* –" and Dancy says her name like it's an accusation – "but I know how long it took to *make* it."

Jezzie sighs and shakes her head. "That's just a sad thing, someone with a mind that ain't got no room for anythin' but what some preacher says."

"This water ain't sweet," Dancy says, after she's emptied the glass. "It's warm, and it tastes like that plastic jug."

Jezzie reaches over and takes the glass from Dancy. "Closed minded *and* ungrateful," she sighs. "You don't look like someone in a position to be picky about the water she's drinking."

"I ain't ungrateful. But you said –"

"You want more, or is my water not good enough for a close-mind, Bible-thumpin', holy-roller hobo?"

"I'm fine, thank you," Dancy says, though she isn't. She could easily drink another half glass of the water. But the girl's right. It was ungrateful, saying what she did, and she's too ashamed to ask for more.

I shouldn't even be here. I should be out there on the road. I don't run. I don't get to run.

"That thing in the sky, you seen that before?" Dancy asks.

Jezzie nods and pours more water into the glass, even though Dancy hasn't asked for it. She sets the glass down on the rug, take it or leave it, and then she looks up at the ceiling of the packing crate.

"Yeah," Jezzie answers, "I've seen it lots. People around here been seein' it on and off since I was little. They call it a thunderbird, and a demon, but that ain't what it is."

"It's a dragon," Dancy says.

Jezzie laughs and shakes her head again. "It ain't no damn dragon, girl. There's no such thing as dragons."

Dancy feels her face flush, and she wants to get up and walk out, leave this heathen girl alone with her dead snakes and Godless books. Instead, she picks up the glass and takes another sip. Instead, she asks, "Then what is it, if it ain't no dragon? You're so smart, Jezebel, you tell me what I saw out there."

"Long time ago," Jezzie says, finally taking her eyes off the ceiling of the crate. "Back about seventy million years ago –"

"The world ain't nearly that old," Dancy says.

"– all these parts round here were covered over by a shallow tropical ocean, like the sea down around the Florida Keys. And there were strange animals in the ocean back then, animals that went extinct, and if we were to see them today, we'd call them sea monsters – the mosasaurs, plesiosaurs, giant turtles. And in the sky –"

"But," Dancy interrupts, "when the Flood came, *Noah's* Flood, everything *was* under water, the whole world, for forty days and forty nights."

"Dancy, you want to hear my answer, or you want to talk?" Jezzie asks and crosses her arms. "You asked me a question, and now I'm tryin' to answer it."

Dancy just shrugs and takes another sip of water. After a moment or two, Jezzie continues.

"That was during what's called the Cretaceous Period," she says, "because of how these shallow seas laid down layers of chalk. In Latin, chalk is *creta*."

Sweat rolls down Dancy's forehead and into the corner of her left eye. It stings.

"I asked you about the dragon," she says, squinting, "*not* for a Latin lesson. And chalk doesn't come from the sea."

"Have you ever even *seen* the inside of schoolhouse?"

Dancy rubs her eye, then stops and stares at Jezzie. The girl's glaring back at her. She has the look of someone whose accustomed to being patient, the look of someone who frequently suffers fools, even though she isn't very good at it. It's a very adult look, and it makes Dancy wish she'd never stepped inside the packing crate.

"In the sky," Jezzie says again, "there were animals called pterosaurs, huge flying reptiles, and if you were to run into one today – which you did – yeah, you'd likely call it a dragon." Then she takes the copy of *Prehistoric Life,* opens it, and thumbs through the pages. She quickly finds what she's looking for, then turns the book around so Dancy cans see, too. On Page 169, there's a drawing of a skeleton, the skeleton of a boomerang-headed monster. The skeleton of Dancy's dragon.

"I'm not in any sorta mood to sit here and argue about scripture and science with you, Dancy Flammarion. But you asked a question, and I answered it as best I can."

Dancy takes the book from her and sits studying the drawing.

"'Skeleton of *Puhteranodon,*'" she reads.

"No. You don't say the 'P,'" Jezzie tells her. "The 'P' is silent."

Dancy frowns and shake her head. "Well, now that's just dumb, sticking in a whole letter you ain't even gonna say. That's just foolish."

"You know, you *might* just be the most pig ignorant white girl I ever met."

Sweat drips from Dancy's bangs and spatters the page. "How?" she asks Jezzie.

"How *what?* How'd you ever get so damn pig ignorant?"

"No," says Dancy, not rising to the bait. "I *mean,* how if these things were around so long ago, and they ain't around no more, did one try to eat me not even half an hour ago? You know all this stuff, then you explain, *Jezebel,* how is it that happened?"

"I don't know," Jezzie admits. She leans back against the cot and wipes her face with the dishrag again. "I heard some people say it's the Devil, and that he's haunting us cause of wicked things people do. Others say it's some kind of Indian god the Muskogee Creek used to pray to and make human sacrifices to. The guy runs the 7-Eleven, he says it came outta a UFO from outer space."

"But *you* don't think any of that's true."

Jezzie frowns. She shrugs and takes the book back from Dancy. "No, I don't suppose I do. It's all just superstition and tall tales, that's all it is."

"So...?"

"You askin' me what I believe instead? I thought the stuff *I* believe is against God, and you don't want to *hear* my blasphemin' nonsense."

"It's really hot in here," Dancy says, changing the subject. "I sat out the thunderstorm this morning in an old freight car, and this place might even be as hot as that."

"You get used to it. Where you from, anyway?"

Dancy glances out the bright rectangular space leading back to the August day.

"Down near Milligan, Florida," she says, "place called Shrove Wood. It's in Okaloosa County. You won't have heard of it. No one's heard of Shrove Wood. But that's where I grew up, near Wampee Creek."

"You get homesick?"

Now it's Dancy's turn to shrug. The cicadas are so loud she imagines that sound shattering the sky, and she imagines, too, the chunks of sky falling down and bleeding blue all over the earth. She thinks about the cabin off Elenore Road that she shared with her grandmother and mother, until the fire. The house where she was born and raised.

"Sometimes I do," she says.

"What you doin' out here on the road, then? Why ain't you back home with your people? You a runway?"

And Dancy almost tells her about the seraph, almost says, *My angel, that's why.* She almost tells the girl about the monsters, all the monsters before the dragon and all the monsters still to come, if the seraph is to be believed, and who in their right mind's gonna say an angel's a liar? She's pretty sure even Jezebel wouldn't say that. She might be a heathen who's been led astray from the Word of God by evil books, but Dancy doesn't think she's crazy.

"I ain't no runaway. I didn't have nothin' to run away from."

Which, she knows, isn't exactly true.

"So, where you headed?"

Dancy doesn't answer that. Instead, she asks, "If you don't think all those other people are right about what the dragon is, and you think it's one of them pterosaurs, then you must have an *opinion* about how it's here."

Jezzie fidgets with the laces of her sneakers.

"I got this notion," she says, "but it doesn't make much sense. I mean, I don't think it's very scientific. I try to be scientific, when I believe something."

The cicadas are so loud, Dancy wants to cover her ears.

"Okay, so," Jezzie says, the book in her lap, the waffle-weave dish-rag on the rug next to her, "I'll tell you what I think. But we ain't gonna argue about it. I ain't asking you to believe any of it. I know you won't, but if I tell you, you don't get to tell me I'm goin' to Hell just for thinking it."

"You don't even believe in Hell."

"You don't know that, Dancy Flammarion. You don't know me."

"Fine," Dancy mutters and takes her eyes off the open door. Orange-white after images dance like ghosts about the inside of the packing crate.

"At the end of the Cretaceous Period, something really bad happened. An asteroid – which is like a meteorite, only a lot bigger – it smashed into the Earth, came down right in the Gulf of Mexico, not even so far from here. And it was a *gigantic* asteroid, maybe big as New York City –"

"You ever been to New York City?"

"No, but that ain't the point. This asteroid was enormous, and when it hit the energy released by the explosion was something like two million times more than the largest atomic bomb ever built. You just think of that much energy. You can't even, not really. But it almost wiped out everything alive, killed off all those sea monsters and the dinosaurs – and the pterosaurs. And maybe it did something else."

"Did something else like what?"

"Maybe it was so big an explosion, down there in Yucatan –"

"Where?"

"Yucatan, Mexico."

"But you just said this happened in the Gulf of Mexico."

"You know *why* it's called the Gulf of Mexico?" Jezzie asks, and Dancy doesn't know, so she shuts up. "But here's what I think," Jezzie goes on. "Maybe that explosion was *so* big it ripped a hole in time. A wormhole or tesseract. And that's how the pterosaur gets through. It's interdimensional or something. It ain't supposed to be here, and it's probably confused as all get out, but here it is anyway, because it flew right through that rip in time, maybe at the very instant of the impact, before the blast wave and firestorms and tsunamis got it.

"And, shit, maybe it ain't nothin' more than an echo, a ghost."

For an almost a full minute, neither of them says anything. Finally, Dancy breaks the awkward silence hanging between them.

"You're really just making all this up," she says.

Jezzie frowns again. "I warned you it wasn't very scientific."

And then the throbbing cicada shriek is pierced by the scream Dancy heard back on the road, the cry of the dragon that Jezzie insists isn't a dragon at all. Instinctively, Dancy ducks her head and reaches for her knife; she notices that Jezzie ducks, as well. They both sit staring at the ceiling of the packing crate, tense as barbed wire.

"That was right overhead," Dancy whispers. "Does it do that? Does it follow you back here?"

Jezzie slowly shakes her head. "Never has before."

It didn't follow her, Dancy thinks. *It followed me.*

And then she sees what's in Jezzie's right hand, an old Colt revolver like the one her grandmother kept around to shoot rattlesnakes.

"You know how to use that?" Dancy asks her, as Jezzie thumbs back the hammer. And the sound of the hammer locking into place is so loud that Dancy realizes the bugs in the trees have gone quiet.

"Wouldn't be holding it like this if I didn't."

"Well, how about put it away," Dancy tells her. "I don't like guns."

Again, Jezzie shakes her head, and she keeps her finger on the trigger of the cocked revolver.

"You never did answer my question," she says. "What you doin' out here, if you ain't a runaway and you ain't a hobo?"

The day has grown so still and silent that Dancy thinks she can almost hear the blood flowing through her veins, can almost hear the grubs and earthworms plowing through the soil beneath the crate. She hasn't yet drawn her knife, but her hand's still on the handle, the carved antler cool and smooth against her perspiring palm. She's been meaning to find some leather to wrap around the handle, because sweat and blood make it slippery, but she hasn't gotten around to it.

"I'm goin' someplace," she tells the girl.

"Yeah, and just where might that be, Dancy Flammarion?"

"I don't know yet," Dancy replies. She didn't even have to think about the answer. Unlike most things, it's simple and true.

"I sorta had a feeling you were gonna say something like that."

"I guess I'll know when I get there," Dancy says. "You reckon that thing's still out there? You reckon it's flying around right over our heads?"

"How the hell am *I* supposed to know?" Jezzie asks and frowns.

"Well, you say you know it ain't no dragon, so I thought maybe –"

"Then you thought wrong."

The silence is broken then by the sound of enormous wings, slowly rising and falling, beating at the sky, and both girls hold their breath as the flapping grows farther and farther away, finally fading into the distance.

Softened almost into melody, Dancy thinks, remembering a line from a book her mother once read her about monsters from Mars trying to take over the world. *But God sent germs to stop them.*

…slain by the putrefactive and disease bacteria against which their systems were unprepared; slain as the red weed was being slain; slain, after all man's devices had failed, by the humblest things that God, in his wisdom, has put upon this earth.

And what's the pterosaur – if the girl named Jezebel's right and it is a pterosaur and not a dragon – but another sort of invader, maybe not from another planet, but from another time, and what's the difference? Something evil that should have died in the Flood, when God – in his wisdom – wiped so much evil off the face of Creation.

"Thanks for the water," Dancy says, and she gets to her feet, finally releasing her hold on the handle of the big Bowie knife.

"You ain't goin' back out there," Jezzie says, still whispering. It's not a question.

"You said it ain't never come out here before. That's cause it's here for me, Jezebel, not for you. It's my dragon to fight, not yours."

"You're really crazy as a damn betsy bug, you *know* that?"

All men are mad in some way or the other, and inasmuch as you deal discreetly with your madmen, so deal with God's madmen…

...so deal with God's madmen...

Dancy's mother read her so many books, before the demons finally came for Julia Flammarion, and so many of the books had monsters in them. She sometimes imagines that her mother knew the seraph was coming, so she was preparing her daughter.

"I ain't lettin' you go out there," Jezzie says again, a little louder than before.

"This is what I do, Jezebel," Dancy replies. "I fight dragons."

Jezebel very slowly eases her thumb off the hammer, decocking the gun.

"It ain't a dragon. It's just an animal."

"Thank you for the water," Dancys says again, shouldering her duffel bag.

"If you'll just wait a few hours, it goes away at night. You could wait here with me, and I could read to you, or I could tell you about the big ol' alligator snapper I found last summer down at Chatham Bend. Or I could tell you more about the chalk seas. I've hardly told you anything about the animals. Did you know, they found a dinosaur up at Selma, back in the 1940s? An actual dinosaur. It was a new kind of duck bill. Then they found another one, related to *Tyrannosaurus,* at —"

"I've already stayed too long," Dancy says, interrupting her. "You never should have brought me here. All that's done is put you in danger."

"Jesus," Jezzie whispers, staring at the gun in her hands. "You really goin' out there, ain't you?"

"Don't you blaspheme," Dancy says. "Bad enough you believe all this evolution claptrap, without you gotta also take the Lord's name in vain."

But, truth be told, all Dancy wants to do is sit in the packing crate with this strange, Godless girl, sipping warm water that tastes like a plastic jug and maybe eating some of those graham crackers and pork and beans. She can't even remember the last time she had a graham cracker. She remembers how they taste smeared with muscadine and blackberry preserves, and her mouth fills with saliva.

"Then here," says Jezzie, "you take this," and she offers Dancy the water jug. Dancy doesn't turn it down. She almost asks for some of the crackers, too, but that would be rude, asking for more when you've just been given such a gift.

"You won't need it?" she asks.

"Nah, it ain't that far back home. And here," says Jezzie, "you take this, too. You need it more'n me." And she holds the revolver out to Dancy. The barrel and the cylinder glint faintly in the dim light inside the packing crate.

"How old is that thing anyway?" Dancy asks. "Looks like it could'a been used in the Civil War, it looks so old. Gun that old, it's liable to blow up in your hands."

Jezzie shrugs. "I don't know," she says. "It was my uncle's. But I don't know how old it is. But here, you take it. It's loaded. Six shots, but I ain't got no extra bullets."

"I don't like guns," Dancy says again. "You keep it. I got my knife."

And ain't that how you slay dragons, with sharp blades? Ain't my knife as good as any sword ever was?

"Dancy, if you'll just wait until sundown –"

"Thank you for the water," Dancy says for the third time. "That's what I most need, it's so hot today."

"What you most *need* is some goddamn common sense."

Dancy almost tells her, again, not to take the Lord's name in vain, but what's the point. Ain't no saving this girl, seduced as she is by atheists and evolutionists.

Just be wasting my breath, that's all.

"It was nice meeting you, Jezebel Lilligraven," Dancy says, even if she's not quite sure that's true.

"Just be careful," Jezzie says.

And then Dancy steps out into the sunlight, hardly any less bright or scorching than when she stepped inside the crate, at least an hour before. She looks up at the indifferent sky above the clearing, half expecting to see the dragon, but there's only the white eye of Heaven gazing back down at her. *It can't be later than three o'clock,* she thinks. *Still hours and hours left until dusk.*

The cicadas are singing again.

When she reaches the edge of the clearing, she looks back just once, and there's the girl's face peering out through a part in the calico curtain. She looks frightened; she waves at Dancy, and Dancy waves back.

I'm never gonna see you again, and I kinda wish that wasn't true.

She walks back into the short stretch of forest dividing the clearing from the road. The going seems a little more difficult than when Jezzie was dragging her along, pell-mell, and she once she gets turned around in a kudzu patch, has to retrace her steps, and find a clearer path. She's drenched in sweat by the time she reaches the gravel shoulder of the highway, and she opens the jug and takes a long swallow. Then she looks again at the blue, blue sky, all the morning's thunderheads come and gone. There's no sign of the dragon, so maybe the girl in the crate was right, and maybe it's flown away back through a hole in time to a world of serpent haunted seas, before Adam and Eve were driven out and cherubim with flaming swords were placed at the gates of Eden that no man or woman would ever again get in. Maybe that's how it is.

And maybe that girl named after a whore and an idolater is right about all of it, and maybe you don't know nothin' about how things really are.

Dancy pushes the thought away, because self doubt's as dangerous as books that say people evolved from monkeys and slime. Self doubt's a distraction that can get her killed. She spares one more glance at the summer sky, and then she starts walking again, following the white center line, which will just have to do as a road map until the angel decides to speak to her again.

DANCY VS. THE PTEROSAUR

This is one of those tales where the title came to me before the actual story. At first, it seemed too goofy to lead anywhere worth going. But I followed it anyway, and it was kinda fun trying to teach Dancy Flammarion a little geology and paleontology, even if she refused to believe a word of it.

Tupelo
(1998)

1.

The albino girl named Dancy Flammarion sits in the psychiatrist's office, in a chair with one leg that's shorter than the other three, so that it wobbles slightly whenever she happens to lean forward. Outside, it's a bright day in late May, and while the psychiatrist talks Dancy half listens and watches as the sun spills in warm through the window, through the open slats of the plastic Venetian blinds, and traces a yellow-white path across the blue wall to her right. The wall with the door that leads out to the hallway and the receptionist and the waiting room and then the hallway that leads down a short flight of stairs and back into the real world. Dancy decided some time ago that the psychiatrist's office isn't precisely part of the real world, but is located, instead, in a crack between sleeping and wakefulness, between one dose of her meds and the next, between night and day. Between breaths and heartbeats. There is nothing about this room, she thinks, that has committed itself to being one thing or another; it never takes a side. Everything here exists between. But the sun, being an eye of God, can get in without an appointment. If the window were open, maybe other things could get in as well, things that know the trick of riding sunbeams – the noise of the traffic out on

Highland Avenue, the sound of robins and blue jays singing, the footsteps and conversations of passing pedestrians. But the psychiatrist has never opened the window, and Dancy has begun to wonder if that's even a possibility or if maybe the architects who designed this in-between place made it so the windows can't ever be opened, not even by the psychiatrist.

"But you understand now that it's only a dream? A dream and a hallucination?" the psychiatrist asks her, and Dancy looks away from the horizontal stripes of sunlight on the blue wall, blinking, looking back at the psychiatrist, trying to recall the answer that's expected of her, the answer that will get her out of the room the quickest. "Animals don't talk," says the psychiatrist, prompting Dancy, because she has other crazy people to see before she can also leave the in-between place and go to wherever it is she lives when she isn't here. Dancy wonders what awful sin the psychiatrist has committed that she's condemned to spend five days a week here in the in-between place.

"I know that," Dancy replies, folding her hands in her lap and making an effort to sit up a little straighter in the wobbly chair.

"They communicate with one another, of course," says the psychiatrist. "But they don't speak to us in human languages."

Dancy nods and manages half a smile. She suspects that the psychiatrist's greatest sin, the one that she will never confess because she's much too prideful (which, of course, is another sin), is her ability to make everything she says seem completely reasonable, no matter how wrongheaded or absurd or at odds with the evidence at hand it might be. That's why she's allowed to sit behind the desk and ask questions and write prescriptions. That's why she was given a key to the room in between. There are framed pieces of paper on the wall that testify to the psychiatrist's powers. Dancy doesn't know much else about the woman. Her name is Dr. Georgia James and, like Dancy, she was born in Florida, and, like Dancy, she has come to live in Birmingham, Alabama, though surely by a very different route. Dr. James wears her hair tied back in a bun or, less often, a braid, and her eyes are almost the same shade of green as Coca-Cola bottles. She's not old, but she's hardly young, either. She keeps her nails polished, and there's always a jar of ribbon candy on her desk, though she's never offered Dancy a piece. She has the most beautiful cursive handwriting that Dancy has ever seen.

"The dog is only a dream I have sometimes," says Dancy. "Or only something I imagine I see when I'm off my meds. I know that now. Because dogs don't talk. Not to us. Not in English. Not in words. Dogs don't follow people down the road singing hymns. Animals don't talk. Birds can't talk, either." And here she wants to mention two exceptions from the Bible – the snake in the Garden of Eden and the donkey in the Book of Numbers – but she doesn't. The psychiatrist might take that the wrong way, and there's only fifteen minutes left on Dancy's hour.

Dr. James makes her approving face and says, "Last summer, the first time you came to see me, you said the dog followed you all the time, everywhere you went, that it would never be quiet and leave you alone. You told me that the dog was the real reason you bought the gun. You remember that?"

"Yeah," Dancy says, "I remember all that. The black dog would never let me sleep. I was getting sick from never sleeping, because the dog kept me awake, talking and singing and going on all the time. I mean, that's how it seemed to me, that the dog didn't want me to ever sleep again. That the dog was able to talk and sing, and that I could hear it. That I couldn't stop hearing it."

"You were sick from all the alcohol and the methamphetamine," the psychiatrist says, her expression changing only slightly. "There was never a talking dog. But you know that, don't you? We've made a lot of progress since the first time I saw you. You should be proud of that. And you should be proud of the fact that you've been clean and sober for so long now."

"I am," she says, because this is what she's supposed to say when there's only fifteen minutes left, whether it's strictly true or not. This is what the psychiatrist needs to hear to let her stand up and leave this in-between place and go back out into the real world. "And I'm grateful, Dr. James. I don't think I've said that often enough, how I'm grateful to you for making me better."

"You made yourself better, Dancy," Dr. James tells her. "All I did was point you in the right direction and give you a little push, see that you got the treatment you need. You're the one who had to do all the heavy lifting."

"I know," says Dancy, and she glances at the clock again, and then looks back at the sun on the blue wall and the office door. She wonders, not for the first time, why the sunlight doesn't burn the walls, the way it's supposed to burn vampires. And she wonders, too, why the architects were allowed to put in a window, unless it's only there to taunt her, like the candy jar on the desk. That all makes sense, but it still surprises her that the sun doesn't sear the walls and leave ugly burns everywhere it touches the paint and plaster, that the walls don't cringe and recoil from its touch.

"Is the new apartment working out?" the psychiatrist asks, taking her white prescription pad from the top drawer of her desk. "Are you settling in okay?"

Dancy starts to point out how the psychiatrist asks her this same question every single time they meet, that Dr. James has asked her if the new apartment's working out at least a dozen times now over the course of the last dozen or so months and it's hardly her new apartment anymore. But instead, like every time before, Dancy just nods and says, "Yes, it is. I like it." And then she adds, "It's quieter than the halfway house was. I can sleep better. I'm getting a lot more sleep." This isn't true, but she's long since learned that truth isn't the shortest distance between two points, especially not when the psychiatrist is involved.

"No trouble with the neighbors?"

"No trouble at all," Dancy lies, and she takes her eyes off the wall and smiles for Dr. Georgia James once again. "At night, I can hear the trains in the distance, passing through the city."

"Is that a bad thing? Don't they keep you awake or wake you up?"

"No," she says. "They remind me of home. It's a safe, familiar sound, the wheels on the rails, the clack of steel against steel, the train whistles. It's almost like listening to my own heartbeat." And at least none of this is a lie, so it's nothing she'll need to feel guilty about later on, nothing she'll need do penance for.

The psychiatrist puts down her prescription pad and leans back in her chair, regarding Dancy more carefully, a bit more closely, than she did only a moment before.

"You think about home a lot these days?" she asks.

"Not a lot," she says, and there's another lie. "But sometimes at night I do, when things are still and quiet, except for the trains."

"And that doesn't make you feel bad? It doesn't make you homesick?"

Dancy keeps smiling, keeping up the act, the brave and expected face, though she wants to curse herself for slipping up like that, for mentioning the trains and how they comfort her, when all it's done is give the psychiatrist a perfectly good reason to be suspicious and ask more questions and try and catch her in a lie. The appointment ends in only ten more minutes. Right now, Dr. James should be writing the prescriptions, and Dancy should be getting ready to say goodbye and thank you and I'll see you next time, next month, getting ready to stand up and leave the office and go back out into the real world. But instead, Dr. James is watching her now like this might be one of the times that the clock gets ignored and whoever she's supposed to see next will just have to wait a while longer. The expression on the psychiatrist's face reminds Dancy of a cat, the expression on a cat's face when something it's been torturing and thinks that it has finally killed unexpectedly moves again – a mouse or a sparrow or a little green anole lizard.

That's me, she thinks. *I'm that little green lizard lying half dead in the grass, and I was trying so hard to be still and play all the way dead, but I twitched. I went and twitched, and now it sees me again. Now it knows there's more fun to be had. Now it knows its work isn't finished yet.*

"I'm not homesick," Dancy says, trying to sound convincing without trying too hard. "The trains make me think of home, that's all. That doesn't mean I'm homesick. That's not what I said."

The psychiatrist nods. "No," she says. "That's not the word you used. You said they remind you of home and that being reminded of home is a comfort. 'A safe, familiar sound.' That's how you put it, wasn't it?"

"I guess so," Dancy says, and then she looks directly at the window for the first time today. It's something she always tries to avoid, because she hates the way the plastic blinds carve the sky, the buildings, the power lines into slices like bacon and because she doesn't want the psychiatrist to know that what is always first and foremost in her mind during their sessions is escaping outside again.

"What I'm getting at, Dancy, is that it follows from what you've told me that you don't feel safe here, in this city, in your apartment, that you don't think of it as your home if hearing the trains inspires in you comforting thoughts of someplace where you lived before. Do you understand what I'm saying?"

"Yes, I understand what you're saying," she replies. "It's not true, but I understand what you mean. I wasn't trying to give you the impression that I'm homesick."

The psychiatrist reaches for the ballpoint pen that she should be using to write out the prescriptions; she taps it smartly several times against the edge of her desk. *Tap, tap. Tap, tap, tap,* and that makes Dancy think of a bird at a windowpane, hungry or cold and wanting inside, and she quickly turns away from the window looking out on

Highland Avenue, because the last thing she needs is to *see* a bird there, a bird that she's only imagining, a bird that isn't any more real that the shaggy black dog that used to follow her and sing "Nearer My God to Thee" and "What a Friend We Have in Jesus."

She can feel the psychiatrist's eyes on her, like sunlight on a blue wall in a place that only exists in between.

"Part of your recovery process," says Dr. Georgia James, "a crucial part, it's accepting that there's nothing for you back there, that there never was, only pain and suffering and disappointment, only people who want to hurt you for who and what you are, people who never loved you and never will. That's what made you sick in the first place. What caused you to run away to Birmingham and turn to drugs and alcohol, what made you hurt yourself and made your mental problems so much worse than they would have been otherwise, the depression and anxiety, the delusions and intrusive thoughts. All of it. I was hoping you had come to accept that, but now I'm not so sure."

"I just like listening to the trains," Dancy tells her, speaking hardly above a whisper. "Honestly, that's all I meant to say."

"Yes, I know. But often it's not what we *mean* to say that matters, but what we *actually* end up saying, instead. I've told you that before, how sometimes we say the truest things of all without ever intending to."

And there's nothing now left for Dancy but to agree with the psychiatrist, and there's no one and nothing to blame but herself. She should have chosen her words more carefully. She should have been more vigilant. She should not have allowed herself to become distracted by the noises getting in from outside, and she certainly shouldn't have ever mentioned the trains. The trains were supposed to be her secret, after all. So, when Dr. James says she thinks they should meet again next week, instead of waiting until May and her next scheduled appointment, Dancy agrees, and then she sits quietly and stares at her hands folded in her lap while the psychiatrist finds a day and a time that's available.

"Will next Thursday afternoon at three work for you?" she asks, and Dancy says yes, sure, next Thursday afternoon is fine.

"Very good," says Dr. James, smiling again. "And if you need me before then, please call. You know that you can call me anytime." And then she writes the prescriptions for haloperidol and clonazepam and gabapentin and tells her not to worry about the trains, that this really isn't too much of a setback, nothing she should lose sleep over. The psychiatrist slides the three pieces of paper across the desk to her, and the sharp black hands of the clock on the wall finally reach four and twelve and the end of the hour. Out on the street, a car or a truck blows its horn and someone shouts angrily, and Dancy says goodbye and is allowed to leave the blue room and return to the real world.

2.

For dinner, Dancy takes a red and white can of Campbell's condensed alphabet soup down from the cabinet and warms it on the tiny gas range in the cramped kitchen of the efficiency apartment that someone at the halfway house found for her. She pays the rent with the checks that come once a month from home – from the place that used to be her home, but, if Dr. James is right, never can be again. The checks are drawn on the Gulf Coast Community Bank in Pensacola and signed by her mother, and they're printed on paper almost the exact same shade of blue as the walls of the psychiatrist's office and are decorated with seashells and sand dollars. There has never yet been anything else in the envelopes that bring the checks, never even so much as a hastily written note. Once, when she mentioned this to Dr. James, the psychiatrist told her she ought to be grateful for the money, but not to expect much more than that, not after everything she's put her family through. Dancy doesn't have a bank account, but there's a place a few blocks away that cashes the checks for a fee, and she keeps all her money in a Red Diamond coffee can in the freezer, hidden behind bags of frozen corn and okra.

When the soup is hot, she pours half of it into a bowl and carries the bowl and a pack of saltine crackers to the table by the window that looks north out across the city. It's the only table anywhere in the apartment, and, like the rest of the furniture, it came with the place. The window is open, and the air getting in smells like cooling asphalt and wisteria, like kudzu and, more faintly, the garbage dumpster in the parking lot. While she waits for her soup to cool, Dancy stares out at the twilight gathering itself like a blue-grey wool blanket across the streets and rooftops. The redbrick building she lives in was built in 1916 and is perched high up on the side of Red Mountain. From here she can see all of Southside and most of downtown, on a clear day almost all the way to the other side of Jones Valley. When her grandfather was a young man, back in the fifties, he'd left Florida for a few years and worked in the Birmingham steel mills. The picture he'd painted whenever he'd happened to talk about the city had made it out to be a place of smoggy skies and black soot, the nights tinged orange-red from the fires and molten steel of the blast furnaces and rolling sheds. The way he'd described it, Birmingham could almost have passed for the outskirts of Hell. But that was a long, long time ago, more than forty years come and gone, and since then most of the mills have closed down. These days, the smog is merely a thin veil of silver grey and comes mainly from the exhaust pipes of all the cars and trucks streaming to and fro along the highways and interstates that crisscross the city.

Sometimes, she thinks that she'll get a cat, or a kitten, so she won't be so alone, but Dr. James has cautioned her against taking on that sort of added responsibility. "Don't you think you have enough to worry about as it is," she asked, "just caring for yourself and staying clean?" And Dancy didn't know what else to do but agree that yes, the psychiatrist was probably right. So, she lives alone in the tiny apartment, only a kitchen and a bathroom, one closet and this small room where she sleeps and eats and reads books that she gets from the library or buys cheap at the Salvation Army thrift store. She has a radio, and there's a twelve-inch black-and-white Zenith television with a bent coat hanger for an antenna that also came with the apartment, but it rarely ever works. And, anyway, one of the knobs is missing and the only way to change channels is with a pair of pliers, which she doesn't own, and reception is so unpredictable that buying them seems like a waste of good money when she doesn't have money to waste.

The plaster walls of the apartment are hidden beneath thick coats of shiny off-white latex paint that, in a certain light, seems almost yellow. In places, the newer paint has blistered and flaked away, revealing earlier, more colorful strata underneath, layers of pale blue, mint green, and, in the kitchen, a rusty shade of red. The ceiling is water-stained, and there's a spot in the bathroom that sags a little.

Dancy eats her alphabet soup and looks out the window and listens to the sounds of the day coming to an end.

Down on the street, two black teenagers are tossing a soccer ball back and forth to one another and talking about girls loudly enough that Dancy can make out at least every other word. The boys live with their mother on the first floor, and their names are Darnell and Tyrone. Their mother has a job with the electric company, but Dancy doesn't know her name. In fact, she doesn't know the names of most of the other people who live in the redbrick building, just the two kids and her next-door neighbors – the old man who rents the northwest corner apartment and the two women who have the northeast corner apartment. The old man's name is Jubal Watts, and he's very, very old and extremely thin, and, like Dancy, he's an alcoholic. Unlike her, he's drunk most of the time. He says that he fought the Japanese in World War II, but Dancy has no way of knowing if that's the truth or not. He's certainly old enough that she supposes it could be. His clothes are always filthy, and he reeks of body odor, bad teeth, stale tobacco, and cheap wine. She's complained to Dr. James about him, because it doesn't seem like the smartest idea, that she should be expected to live next door to an old wino when she's trying so hard to stay sober. But the psychiatrist told her she should be grateful that she has somewhere to live, what with her having a criminal record and all, and, anyway, if the man's a war veteran she should be more respectful. And Dancy thinks that maybe that's true, but, then again, maybe it's not.

It took her awhile to realize that the two women who live in the apartment on the northeast corner of the building are lesbians. One evening when she went to take the trash down, their door was standing wide open, and Dancy saw them sitting together on their sofa, dressed in nothing but their underwear. They were kissing. It isn't like she was spying on them. It's not like that at all. Actually, it almost seemed to Dancy that they'd *wanted* her to see them, that they'd known she would be coming down the hallway right about then, because she always takes her trash down at pretty much the same time, twice every week, late on Thursday afternoons and late Monday afternoons. They looked up and saw her, and Dancy quickly turned her head away and hurried along to the stairs at the end of the hall. After that, she realized that sometimes she could hear them having sex and that she'd been hearing them ever since she moved in, but it hadn't occurred to her exactly what she was hearing. Growing up in Muscogee, a town not far from Pensacola, she hadn't known any gay men or lesbians, and she'd been raised to believe that such things were wicked and unnatural and against God. But she'd also been raised to believe that drunks and drug addicts and people who abandon their children and pull guns on convenience-store cashiers are wicked, and she was guilty on all four of those counts, wasn't she? And hadn't Jesus said in the Book of John to let those among you who is without sin cast the first stone? So Dancy didn't say anything about them to the psychiatrist. For all she knew, the psychiatrist is also a lesbian. There are no photos of a husband or any kids in her office, and maybe that's why. One of the next-door lesbians is a pretty girl, a blonde named Cheryl, but the other is mannish and heavy set and has short hair the color of a dead mouse. Her name is Jo. Or maybe she spells it Joe. Dancy has never asked, and it's not like she's going to go peeking at their mail to try and find out. It's none of her business. None of it is, not after the life she's lived and the things she's done. People who live in glass houses shouldn't throw rocks, as her grandmother used to say, and if ever anyone lived in a house made of glass, Dancy thinks she must certainly be that person, the way the world around her feels ready to shatter at any moment.

Dancy finishes her soup and crackers, then sits staring out the window at the street and the parking lot and the rear of South Highland Presbyterian Church on the other side of the parking lot, watching as dusk becomes night and the streetlights wink on. Darnell and Tyrone's mother has called them inside to their own suppers. There are a few fireflies out tonight, flickering chartreuse pinpoints in the gathering dark. Fireflies are one of the things she misses most about living in the country; she rarely sees them anymore, unless she walks the three blocks down to Magnolia Park at sunset, and even there among the trees they're scarce.

The weather's been warm enough the last couple of weeks that Dancy has been able to leave the sashes up all night long, but not yet so warm that she's had to close them and start running the cranky window-unit air conditioner that, like the furniture and the broken television, came with the apartment. It makes terrible, wet, wheezing noises that Dancy imagines is what it would sound like if maybe a robot were dying of pneumonia or tuberculosis, and it drips so much from all the condensation that she has to keep the mop bucket on the floor beneath it. Worse still, once June rolls around and the real summer heat begins, it does a piss-poor job of keeping the place cool enough for comfort. This will be Dancy's second summer in the apartment, and last year there were nights she couldn't get to sleep for the heat. And so she'd lie awake until dawn, staring at the water stains, smelling her own sweat, thinking about things she shouldn't.

She's about to get up and take her bowl over to the sink and start washing the dishes when she spots the black dog crossing the parking lot, loping along in the space between one streetlight and the next. It's probably one of the biggest dogs she's ever seen. Her grandfather raised bloodhounds, but this dog is bigger than that, so maybe it's part Great Dane or Rottweiler or something. It's trotting along with its head held low, its nose hovering just above the asphalt, as if the dog is following a scent, tracking something or someone. She imagines that she can even hear its claws clicking against the pavement and the sound of its hot breath, not so different from the wet sounds that the old air conditioner makes.

"No," she says, and then Dancy shuts her eyes tightly, and she says, "I'm not hearing it, and I'm not seeing it, either. It isn't real, and even if it is real, it's only a stray or someone's pet dog that should be on a leash, but isn't. There are leash laws, but not everybody obeys the law, do they? And sometimes dogs get out when no one's looking. You open the door, and they dash right past you, despite your best intentions. It's not there, or it's just a plain old regular dog. It's just a dog, if it's even there at all." And then she counts to thirty, just like the psychiatrist said she should, and when Dancy opens her eyes again there's no sign of the animal. She sits at the window for another minute or so, staring down at the parking lot, and she thinks that maybe tomorrow she'll ask Darnell and Tyrone if they've seen a big black dog hanging around. She thinks she probably should, just to be safe, if she happens to see the boys tomorrow, because if it were a real dog, it could be dangerous. It might not have had its shots.

"But probably it wasn't there at all," she says, trying to hear Dr. James speaking the words, because everything seems more reasonable coming from the psychiatrist. And then Dancy takes her bowl and her spoons and the rest of the pack of saltine crackers and turns her back on the open window.

3.

That night while she's sleeping the dog comes back to Dancy Flammarion.

In the dream, she's alone and walking east on a dark country road, a road she thinks she might recognize if it were day, instead of being sometime well past midnight. In her right hand she's carrying a tattered umbrella, folded shut, and in her left hand, she carries a small suitcase that weighs so little that it must surely be empty. It isn't just any suitcase. It's her mother's denim-blue Lady Baltimore, the one she got for her sixteenth birthday, the one she let Dancy use the two years she went away to church summer camp up in Andalusia. There's a makeup mirror glued to the inside of the lid, and the suitcase is lined in chameleon satin that shifts from periwinkle to lavender, depending on the light. The latches are rusty, and the key was lost a long time ago. Dancy sets the suitcase down and looks back the direction she's come. The narrow two-lane highway recedes into the darkness, stretching away to the vanishing point, an asphalt ribbon divided by a broken white line, flanked on either side by the trunks of strangled pines draped in the impenetrable vines and huge heart-shaped leaves of kudzu plants. Together, the dead trees and the kudzu form towering walls that make it impossible for her to tell anything more about the landscape around her. It could be farmland or forest, swamps or wild prairie, there's no way to know. Overhead, the night is ablaze with more stars than she can remember ever having seen all at once on a single night. There's no moon, though, so either tonight's a new moon or it's already set or hasn't yet risen. The air is humid and thick as breakfast gravy, weighed down with all the smells of a hot summer night, with the scent of kudzu flowers and pine sap and the puddles of tar that melted during the day and have only just begun to get hard again. All around her the darkness is still and silent, save for the chirping of peep toads and crickets from the kudzu. Wherever she is, she must be nowhere near a town.

All of this, it's a familiar dream, this long road beneath the Southern stars. It's a place Dancy's come back to in her sleep so many times that her waking self has long since lost count. But for now, in this moment, she has no recollection of ever having stood here before. Here inside the dream, she has no awareness that she is, in fact, dreaming, any more than she can remember why she's on this road or where it might possibly lead. But her feet hurt, and she's sleepy, and she feels as if it has been a very long time since she's had anything at all to eat. Her clothes are filthy, and she stinks of old sweat. Somewhere among the dead pines and kudzu snarl, a hoot owl calls out, and it seems like just about the loneliest sound Dancy has ever heard.

"Well, you can't just stand here all night," she says out loud to herself, picking up her mother's blue suitcase, and she starts walking again, never mind her aching feet or not knowing where it is she's bound. Maybe, she thinks, if she stops trying so hard to remember how she got here it will all come back to her, just like when she misplaces her billfold or her reading glasses. She thinks maybe she'll count the stars and distract herself by looking for constellations – the Big Dipper, Cassiopeia, Orion, the Pleiades. But Dancy hasn't taken more than eight or nine steps when the enormous shaggy black dog comes bounding out of the kudzu, only a little ways up ahead of her, and she stops dead in her tracks. It might possibly be the biggest damn dog that she's ever seen. It stops at the edge of the highway and stands there staring at her, then glances up at the stars, as if it also has an interest in the constellations, as if possibly it were reading Dancy's mind. She can hear her heart beating, and her mouth has gone dry. The dog shakes itself, gives a loud woof, and then begins trotting towards her, its claws making a staccato snicking sound against the highway.

Dancy turns to run, no thought now but to get away from the dog, and didn't she hear a story once about wild dogs taking down a full-grown Brahman bull, and hasn't she also heard tales of them stealing babies and little kids and killing people? She turns expecting nothing but hungry darkness and the empty road stretching off between those high walls of kudzu, and instead there are the bright headlights of an oncoming car that she's almost certain wasn't there only a moment or two before. She drops the tattered umbrella and her mother's suitcase and frantically waves her arms for the driver to stop; she can worry later on if hitchhiking is the lesser of two evils, the frying pan or the fire.

The driver puts on his brakes and pulls off onto the weedy shoulder of the road. The tires crunch gravel and pine straw. It's a great scabby land yacht of a car that's seen better days, an Oldsmobile that's as much rust and Bondo as it is whatever color it used to be painted. The driver shifts into neutral, and the engine protests, makes an ugly grating noise. Dancy looks over her shoulder, and the shaggy black dog has stopped, but it's still there, watching her, watching the car. Caught in the headlights, its eyes flash a metallic iridescent green like the wings of june bugs.

The fat man driving the car leans his bald head out the open window and he says, "Girl, you gonna stand there all night while that beast makes up his mind or you gonna get a wiggle on. It so happens I got other places to be and other people to see." There's almost as much rumble in his voice as there is in the Oldsmobile's engine.

"Okay," says Dancy, "I'm coming." And she gathers up her belongings and hurries around to the passenger-side door, picking her way through waist-high goldenrod and Queen Anne's lace. The bald man tells her to put the suitcase in the back seat, and she does. Then he tells her to lock the door, and she does that too. When she looks again, the dog's gone, vanished back into the kudzu. Or just vanished.

The bald man shifts the car into drive and pulls onto the highway again. "You gotta be careful of strays," he says and rubs at his scraggly beard. Dancy thinks that it's more the sort of beard that comes from repeatedly forgetting to shave than from trying to grow one on purpose. The inside of the car stinks of wintergreen chewing tobacco and menthol cigarettes. There's also an air-freshener shaped like a pine tree dangling from the rearview mirror, but Dancy can't smell that at all.

"Thank you, Mister," she says, as they pass the place where the dog had been standing, and she checks to be sure her door's locked.

"You ain't gotta thank me for giving you a lift. What was I gonna do? Keep going and leave you to fend for yourself?" And he spits tobacco juice into a 7-Eleven Big Gulp cup.

"Lots of folks would've," she replies. "People are like that."

"You seem awful young for a cynic," says the bald man, and then he stares at her for a bit, instead of keeping his eyes on the road. "You're an actual genuine albino, ain't you?"

Instead of answering the question, because it was rude, and, besides, it should be perfectly obvious to anyone who isn't blind that's she an albino, Dancy says, "I'm twenty-three. That ain't so young, not these days."

"Twenty-three, huh? Me, I wouldn't have guessed you're much more than sixteen. Hell, maybe not even that. Where you headed, anyway? I didn't pass any broke-down cars back there, so I don't think you're walking 'cause of a flat or a busted radiator or 'cause you went and run outta gas."

"No, I didn't break down," she says, but she's thinking that maybe she did, and that's part of what she can't remember. Maybe she did, but he just didn't notice her car, or maybe she walked to the highway from a side road or something.

"Then you're a hitcher," he concludes, and Dancy doesn't bother denying it. "So, where you headed?" the bald man asks again. "Ain't nothing much on this road until you get to Faceville, and, come to think of it, ain't nothing much to Faceville, either. Maybe you're going all the way to Bainbridge?"

"Yeah," she says, because it seems like a better idea than saying she doesn't know where she's going. "I got an aunt and uncle and cousins in Bainbridge."

"Is that a fact? An aunt and uncle and cousins, and here you're taking time to visit, but they couldn't see fit to give you the money for a bus ticket?"

"I don't like buses," she says, which is true, even if it isn't much of an explanation. "I don't like the crowds on buses, and I don't like the diesel fumes."

The bald man spits into his plastic cup again, then says, "I reckon you wouldn't much like getting chewed alive by that dog back there, neither. It don't always pay to be so persnickety about the means of our conveyance through this world."

"I don't like riding buses, that's all."

"So you told me."

Dancy steals a quick glance over her shoulder, as if maybe she thinks the dog is following them, chasing the car down the road, but there's nothing to see back there but the reddish glow of the taillights reflected off the asphalt.

"Is that where you're going, Bainbridge?" she asks the bald man.

"Me? No, no, I'm afraid not. I'm going to Savannah, with a stop in Valdosta on the way, and I'm rather partial to staying off the beaten path, if you catch my drift. Bainbridge, it ain't on my itinerary tonight. If you still mean to go to Bainbridge, I'm afraid I can't take you no farther than Faceville and the junction with Bettstown Road. That'll put you about eleven miles south of Bainbridge. Likely as not, you can catch another ride from there or walk the difference and take your chances with that mutt."

"I've never been to Faceville," she says.

66

"Ain't no reason you should have," the bald man tells her. "Hell, ain't nothing there but a boiled peanut stand, a gas station, and more churches than any two-bit, pissant bend in the highway has a right to. Where you from, anyhow?"

Dancy opens her mouth to say Muscogee, Florida, not too far from Pensacola, but then it occurs to her that maybe telling this man the truth is a bad idea. Maybe the less he knows, the better. "Mobile," she says. "Mobile, Alabama."

"And you done walked all that way here from Mobile, Alabama?" he asks and spits into his cup again.

"Some of it," she replies. "Some of it I rode with a truck driver, but we had a falling out, and I've been walking since just past Chattahoochee."

"Just past Chattahoochee," the bald man says, and he says it like he doesn't believe her. He laughs and nods his head, "Well, all right then. That's as good a tale as any, I suppose. A sight better than some I've heard." And then he switches on the radio, and there's a man singing about Tupelo. The singer's voice is low and somehow threatening and almost as gravelly as the driver's.

It occurs to Dancy that they're still surrounded by the high walls of kudzu, and she starts to ask the driver of the Oldsmobile if he knows how much farther the highway's like this, how long until they'll be out of the kudzu and in open country. But instead, and for no reason she could ever put her finger on, she asks, "You know something about that dog back there?"

"If you're asking whether I know something about black dogs, then yeah," he tells her, "even if I've never made the acquaintance of that particular black dog. I know they can be omens, if you know how to read omens, if you're paying attention."

"I never heard that," she says.

"Girl, maybe there's a lot you ain't heard," he tells her. "But it's gospel, all the same. Going hundreds of years back, maybe thousands of years back, folks who are wise to signs and portents have known that the appearance of a black dog can be a warning, a harbinger of death and doom. A premonition of evil times, if you will."

"We had a black dog when I was a little kid," Dancy says, watching the kudzu and the darkness rushing by outside the car window, trying not to think about everything that might be hiding in vines, looking out, watching her. "His name was Lockjaw, and he was never a portent of death and doom. I think you made that up."

The driver takes his eyes off the road long enough to stare at her and scowl and scratch at his beard.

"Lockjaw?" he asks her. "What in the Sam Hill kind of name is that for a dog?"

"I didn't name him," Dancy says and shrugs. "My momma did, and she said he was so stubborn as a puppy that if he ever bit into something or someone his jaws would lock up tight and he wouldn't turn loose until he was ready, and you couldn't make him do any different."

"Might as well name a dog Tetanus," the bald man mutters.

"I didn't name him," Dancy says again. "But he was a good dog, Mister, and that's my point. Bad things didn't happen to us because we had a black dog."

"You ain't listening. But, then again, that ain't my problem."

Dancy wants to ask him to turn the radio off, because she doesn't like that song or the way the singer's voice is making her feel. But here this man has given her a ride and saved her from a wild dog, and it doesn't seem right to turn around and complain about what he's playing on his own car radio.

"That's Faceville coming up," he says, and Dancy looks, but all she can see is the kudzu and the highway. She squints, and maybe, just maybe there's a brighter patch of darkness way on ahead of them, just the faintest smudge of light. "The way things are going, you and I, we might not get a chance to talk again. There's lots of folks round here – and I mean the kind of folks it's best not to meddle with, best not to rile – who want to see you six feet under, 'cause of what you done and what you're gonna do."

And that's when she remembers why she's going to Bainbridge, when she realizes telling the bald man that where she's headed wasn't a lie, after all. She'll forget again, just as soon as she wakes up, but right now she knows. Down in her belly, down in her guts, there's a cold heaviness, and she feels the hairs along her arms and on the back of her neck start to prick. On the radio, the singer's voice growls and booms.

Distant thunder rumble, rumble hungry like the Beast.
The Beast it cometh, cometh down. The Beast it cometh, cometh down.
Tupelo bound. Tupelo-o-o. Yeah, Tupelo.
The Beast it cometh, Tupelo bound.

Dancy switches off the radio without bothering to ask the bald man's permission.

"To each their own," he tells her and spits tobacco juice, "but like I done already said, you ain't listening."

"What is it I'm not listening to?" Dancy asks him. "You mean that song? Or that nonsense about black dogs being evil." Her hand is on the door handle now, gripping it tight, and she wonders how much it's gonna hurt when she hits the pavement, if the car's going fast enough that she'll break an arm or leg or worse. She thinks about lying there on the road, crippled and bleeding, while all the things watching from the kudzu take their time deciding what's to be done with her. And she asks him, "What exactly is it you think I need to hear?"

"Anyhow," he says, brushing her questions aside, "if you want my honest to God opinion, I think you're just about the most inter- esting goddamn thing to happen round these parts since – well, maybe since forever. But then, you see, I ain't myself from around these parts, and I don't precisely have a vested interest in how it all shakes out, all the shit you're stirring up. My name ain't on your list, so when it comes right down to brass tacks, it don't much matter to me one way or another. Not except what I done said, that I *do* find you interesting, and things can get awful damn boring out here in the ass end of nowhere. And that's just about plenty enough to make me get off the bench and take a side. But then I always have had a perfidious streak about me, a smidgen of the mercenary soul, if you will."

"I don't know what you're talking about," she says. "But I want you to stop this car and let me out."

"Of course you do," he says, "and of course you don't, and if you give me half a second, I'll oblige. But I'm thinking, next time round, I won't be stopping. Next time, you gotta deal with old Lockjaw back there. And we'll see how that goes."

And then the bald man pulls his rusty Oldsmobile over and lets her out of the car, and Dancy watches him drive off, watches until the taillights are just pinpricks, dimmer than all those stars twinkling overhead. She's about to pick up the blue Lady Baltimore suitcase and her umbrella and resume her long walk down Highway 97 towards Bainbridge when the dream ends, and she comes awake in a sweat-soaked tangle of sheets. It's almost sunrise, and the sky outside her window is the color of a bruise. She lies there staring up at the water-stained ceiling above her bed, listening to her heart and to the noise of the garbage truck's hydraulic lift picking up the dumpster and the week's worth of trash in the dumpster. She tries hard to remember everything about the dream, because this time something was different, and she should write it down for the psychiatrist. But the details come apart and slip away from her, and by the time the garbage truck is done and pulls away from the brick building on the side of Red Mountain, all that's left behind is the memory of the road and the kudzu and blazing star-filled Heaven above it all.

4.

A long and mostly unremarkable week passes, and then it's Thursday again, and Dancy is sitting in the wobbly chair in the psychiatrist's office, staring at slices of bright sunlight on the blue walls of this room that exists somewhere in a crack between sleeping and wakefulness. She's having a little trouble paying attention and keeping up with the questions that Dr. Georgia James has been asking her, but that's probably just because of the gabapentin or the haloperidol. Sometimes her meds made her groggy and make it difficult to read or even follow the plot of a TV show. She's complained about the side effects before, but her complaints are always met with the same assurances that, in time, sooner later, those unpleasant symptoms will fade. Besides, isn't being a little sleepy or confused better than being so crazy that you buy a gun and kidnap your own daughter and drive her all the way to Tupelo, Mississippi before the police finally catch up with you?

That's what they've been talking about for the past fifteen minutes – the long drive and Dancy being so selfish and short-sighted that she'd put other people's lives in danger. She's the one who brought it up. The psychiatrist asked what was on her mind this afternoon, and Dancy admitted that she was thinking about Tupelo, because just the day before she got a surprise visit from her parole officer, and those always dredge up bad memories. Somehow, though, even talking about Tupelo is better than being told that it's a bad thing that she's comforted by the sound of trains, which, of course, is supposedly the reason she's having to see the psychiatrist today, instead of next month. But so far, Dr. James hasn't even bothered to mention the trains, which makes Dancy wonder if that was really the psychiatrist's reason for making her come back so soon. Maybe that was never it at all. Maybe, Dancy thinks, the psychiatrist knew that her parole officer was planning to show up unannounced on Wednesday morning, and that's the *real* reason that she made Dancy come back three weeks early. She rubs her eyes and forces herself to stop staring at the sun on the wall.

"I smell kudzu all the time," she says, changing the subject. "I mean, I've started smelling kudzu all the time, just the last few days. Since the last time I saw you."

"Well, that's not so strange," the psychiatrist tells her. "There's a lot of the stuff growing around here."

"Not in my bathroom there's not," Dancy replies. "And not in the Piggly Wiggly or Woolworth's, either. There's no kudzu growing in Magnolia Park or at the library."

"No," agrees Dr. James. "No, there isn't."

"I've started smelling it everywhere I go. Most times, it doesn't bother me. Most times, I hardly even notice it, until all of a sudden I do, and then I can't stop noticing it. I thought maybe it was another side effect from my medication. I thought you could tell me if that's all it is or if maybe it's something else. When I was a kid, I had an uncle who started smelling things that weren't there, like coffee and crape myrtle flowers, and it turned out that he had a brain tumor, and he died of it."

The psychiatrist leans forward and taps at the cover of a book on her desk with the eraser end of a yellow pencil. "I don't think you have a brain tumor," she says. "I seriously doubt it's anything you should be worried about. Probably, if you stop worrying about smelling kudzu, you'll stop smelling it. It's possible you're experiencing a mild olfactory hallucination, because of your schizophrenia. They're relatively rare with your type of the disease, but it does occur. Yes, I suspect that's all it is."

"But it's never happened to me before," Dancy tells her.

"There's always a first time for everything, isn't there?"

Dancy nods, because yes, of course there is, and she tries to remember the first time she walked into the psychiatrist's office, the first time she sat in the wobbly chair and stared at the sun shining through the Venetian blinds, washing across the blue walls of the room. But she can't.

"What are you reminded of by the scent of kudzu?" Dr. James asks her.

"Grape jelly," Dancy replies, without having to think about it. "Kudzu has always smelled like grape jelly to me. Like grape jelly and fresh-cut grass."

"No, I'm sorry, that's not what I meant. I'm not asking what kudzu smells like to you, but what the smell of kudzu reminds you of and how it makes you feel."

"This is like the trains, isn't it?"

"Yes," the psychiatrist tells her. "This is very much like the trains."

Dancy sighs and looks down at the toes of her tennis shoes, feeling now like she's screwed up and walked straight into some sort of trap by bringing up the kudzu. But that's often how it seems with the psychiatrist, like trying to navigate a field or vacant lot strewn with snares and booby traps and land mines, having to watch her every footstep and every single word she says. Having to guard against carelessly spoken thoughts and seemingly harmless comments, because if she *doesn't* she can wind up with extra office visits or higher doses of her meds, worried looks and even, once or twice, Dr. James wondering aloud if maybe Dancy isn't ready to be out on her own, after all.

"Why is it that you still don't trust me?" the psychiatrist asks her. "We've been seeing one another for more than a year and a half, but times like now I get the distinct impression that you're still reluctant to place your full confidence in me. Can you tell me why that is, Dancy?" And those words come loaded with accusation, and they come loaded with guilt and reproach. How dare she hide behind walls and keep the psychiatrist at arm's length when Dr. James has tried so hard to help her, above and beyond what she usually does for her patients? How dare she be evasive and pretend like she doesn't understand perfectly well the questions that are being asked?

"I never said that I don't trust you," Dancy replies, and she doesn't look away from the toes of her shoes and the floor, doesn't look up into the psychiatrist's probing bottle-green eyes. "I misunderstood the question, that's all."

"But you understand it now," says the psychiatrist.

"Yes, I understand it now."

"So, tell me, how does the smell of kudzu make you feel?"

Dancy shuts her eyes for a moment and covers her face with both her hands, and she asks herself, *What happens if I don't tell her, if I refuse? What happens if I just say, 'I'm sorry, but I don't want to talk about this anymore.' I'm the one who brought it up, so it's only fair that I should be able to stop talking about it if that's what I want. Maybe if I start talking about the trains, instead.*

"Dancy, are you okay? Would you like some water?"

Dancy uncovers her face and opens her eyes, and for just an instant or so she has the impression that the room has gone dark, as if the sun set when she wasn't looking and now the office is filled with shadows. She blinks and the sun washes back in between the slats of the Venetian blinds and the walls are blue again. *Don't tell her about that, either,* Dancy thinks. *Don't tell her about that most especially.*

"I'm fine," she says and forces herself to lift her chin and look the psychiatrist in the eyes. "That smell, it makes me afraid. Since this started, me smelling kudzu when there isn't any kudzu around to smell, it frightens me. When it happens, I start to feel like I'm suffocating, like someone's holding a pillow over my face and I can't breathe."

"It sounds like your describing a panic attack," the psychiatrist tells her. "We've talked about those."

"No, it isn't like that," Dancy insists, and she very much wants to look away again, because she's realized that the darkness that briefly seemed to swallow the whole room has retreated to the psychiatrist's eyes, and it's coiled there now like two cottonmouth water moccasins, gazing hungrily out at her. If it's never before occurred to Dancy that darkness can be hungry, it does now. But she doesn't look away. Instead, she balls her hands into fists, digging her short nails into her palms.

"How is it different?" the psychiatrist asks. "Can you explain?"

"I almost drowned once," Dancy says, knowing this isn't exactly the answer that Dr. James and the darkness coiled inside her eyes wants to hear, but maybe it can be made to pass for that answer. Maybe if she's lucky and uses just the right words, maybe they won't know the difference.

"They?" Was it always "they?" Have there always been three of us in this room?

"In Muscogee, back home, we used to swim in an old flooded sand pit, not too far from the Perdido River. Me and my cousins and other kids. It was safer than swimming in the river, because there were alligators in the river, but no one had ever seen a gator in the sand pit. I suspect they were probably there, but no one had ever actually *seen* one, you know? Used to, there was a company dug sand from there for cement, and they'd had to keep pumps going day and night, because the water table's so high in Muscogee."

The psychiatrist nods a patient, indulgent sort of nod and leans back in her chair, but Dancy can tell that there's nothing patient nor indulgent about the darkness that's turned Dr. James' green eyes as black as oil. Dancy thinks, *The darkness has heard it all before. The darkness knows the score.* She glances at the clock and sees that there's only twenty minutes remaining in her appointment, and all she has to do is keep talking and tell this story, and before she knows it her time will be up and she'll be back out on the street, under the late May sky where the darkness can't see her.

"But after a few years the company went bust and abandoned the pit, so no one was pumping out the water anymore, and I guess it filled up pretty fast. That was back before I was born, but Momma told me about it. Anyway, that's where we'd go to swim, that pit, and also to look for fossil shark teeth and shells, even though Muscogee is a good twenty miles from the Gulf. This one day when I was eight years old, we were swimming there, and I'd gone way out towards the middle, farther than we were supposed to go, out where the pit was so deep no one could ever find the bottom. And I got a cramp in my leg. I would have drowned, sure as I'm sitting here talking to you, only one of my cousins saw how I was in trouble, and he was the best swimmer of all us kids. He got me back to shore. I don't remember too much about it, really, but I do remember sinking and watching the air bubbles from my mouth and nose racing back up towards the surface. I remember how they reminded me of little jellyfish, the way they shimmered and moved in the water. And I remember what it felt like having no air, and thinking I was never going to have any air ever again, that in a few seconds more the water would rush up my nostrils and into my mouth, and I'd be drowned."

And I remember sinking into the dark, she thinks, but keeps the thought to herself. *How the water turned inky black only a couple of feet down, how that blackness reached up to pull me under, and possibly it wasn't a cramp at all, but just the dark wrapping itself around my leg and holding on.*

"That's what it's like, smelling the kudzu, like that day in the sand pit back home when I nearly drowned. That's exactly how it makes me feel, like I can't get my breath, like I'm never going to be able to breathe again. I'll just keep sinking, maybe forever because maybe there isn't even really a bottom, and the weight of all that water is there to hold me down. That's what the smell of kudzu reminds me of and how it makes me feel."

The psychiatrist nods her head, and then she takes out one of her white prescription pads, and she says, "I want you to try something new, Dancy. Something that's only just been approved by the FDA, and I hear it's especially good with panic attacks. Keep taking your other medication, same as always, but I want you to take this at bedtime. I think it will help."

"But I already take so many pills," Dancy says, and the darkness in the psychiatrist's eyes grins back at her.

"Just give it a try," Dr. James tells her, writing out the script in her neat cursive. "It's new, but it's covered by your Medicare, and there's no reason you should be suffering, not if you don't have to suffer. That's what this is all about, you coming here to talk with me, my helping you stay clean and finding the medication that will make you better. It's about eliminating suffering, the pain you've endured from your illness, all the pain you've caused yourself and others, your little girl and her father and your family back home in Florida. No one has to hurt anymore."

The psychiatrist tears the page off the pad and passes it across the desk to Dancy.

"How about we end things early today? Would that be okay with you?"

Dancy takes the prescription, and "Sure," she says. "It's okay if we end early today. I need to run some errands, anyway. I need to go to the market. I'm almost out of sugar and milk, and I need to buy —"

"Then I'll see you on June 19th," the psychiatrist says, interrupting her. "How does that sound. It's a Friday afternoon. Does that work for you? We could do the 22nd, if you'd rather. That's a Monday."

"No, Friday the 19th is fine."

"Three o'clock okay?"

Dancy nods and glances down at the slip of white paper with the psychiatrist's name and the address of the building where she has her office printed across the top. Dancy blinks, and now it isn't a slip of paper at all, but a heart-shaped kudzu leaf, instead. Then she hears the sound that slips out from between her teeth and across her lips, and it's as if the sound is something she's hearing from the hallway or from another room. It's a small and startled sound, a brittle sound.

A rabbit sound, she thinks.

The kudzu leaf slips from her fingers, then, and it seems to Dancy that it takes a very long time for it to fall. But when it finally settles on the floor by the toes of her shoes, it's only a white slip of paper again.

5.

It wasn't true that she needed to make a trip to the Piggly Wiggly. She isn't low on sugar, and she doesn't need to buy milk. But she does go to the pharmacy, walks all the way to the CVS on 11th Avenue, across from the university, and while she waits for the new prescription to be filled, Dancy wanders the narrow, cluttered aisles and shoplifts a lipstick and an eyeliner, even though she never wears makeup. The lipstick is a deep red, and the sticker on the tube reads "Firefly." If she did wear makeup, she thinks, then she'd certainly wear Firefly lipstick. She also takes a can of tuna, so she doesn't have to feel too guilty about only taking silly, impractical things. No one notices; she learned to shoplift when she was still using and was stealing Sudafed for a meth lab out in Bessemer. When her prescription is ready, she shows the pharmacist her Alabama Medicare card, pays her copay, and walks home, taking the long way so she won't have to pass the bars at Five Points, climbing the steep streets to the redbrick building on the side of the mountain. Once she's safely inside and the door is shut and locked behind her, she puts the tuna in the kitchen pantry, between a can of Campbell's tomato soup and a can of potted meat. The stolen makeup she carries to the bathroom and puts on a shelf inside the medicine cabinet where no one will ever see it.

When she closes the medicine cabinet door, Dancy catches her reflection in the mirror staring back at her. Maybe her birth certificate says she's twenty-three, but this afternoon she could pass for thirty easy, and a hard thirty, at that. Like they say, the years have not been kind to her, the years and the drugs and her months in jail, everything that's happened since her release. She takes a moment to drag a comb through her white hair, because it looks like she hasn't bothered to comb it in days, and suddenly she's embarrassed that she went out like that, that she went to her psychiatrist appointment with her hair almost as tangled as a rat's nest. Her pink-red irises seem brighter than usual, and there are ugly circles beneath her eyes, like she hasn't been sleeping, even though she mostly has. Her pale face, white as chalk dust, is splotchy and there's a zit coming in above her left eye.

Dancy gives up on her hair and goes to the table by the open window, where she sits down and takes the bottle of pills from the white CVS bag. She holds the bottle up, but it's hard to tell much about what's inside through the amber plastic, so she unscrews the cap and pours several pills out into her open hand. They're tiny and round and deep black, the exact same shade of dark as the darkness that had briefly filled Dr. James' entire office, before retreating and taking shelter in her eyes. There are no identifying numbers or letters stamped into the pills, and they feel cold and damp against her hand. Worse, they seem to glisten, and she thinks they glisten the same way oil on a puddle does. She quickly returns them to the bottle, then sets the bottle at the center of the table, next to the salt and pepper and Tabasco sauce, and sits staring at the new prescription. It's only then that she realizes the label pasted onto the bottle is blank. There isn't even the CVS logo. She starts to reach for the pills again, when there's a knock at the door.

No one ever knocks on Dancy's door except when there are surprise visits from her parole officer or when the old man next door shows up offering her five or ten bucks if she'll walk to the liquor store for him. She almost shouts at whoever it is to go away and leave her alone. *Fuck off, Mr. Jubal Watts. If you want that bottle of Mad Dog so bad, you can walk the two blocks your own damn self.* But it might not be Jubal Watts. It might be her p.o. *Or,* she thinks, *maybe someone saw you shoplifting, and it's the police.*

"No," she whispers, "no one saw me, and it isn't the police."

There's another knock, a little more insistent than the first, and she tells herself that maybe it's only the exterminator come to spray for roaches and set out traps for mice, even though he's already come this month. Dancy gets up and goes to the door, because it's safer than the alternative, because not answering the door would likely only make a bad thing worse. A bad thing can always get worse. That's one of the few truths that she's certain she's learned over the years.

"I'm coming," she says, so they won't knock again. Then she slides the chain bolt almost all the way free of the track in the brass plate and asks, "Who is it? Who's there?"

"It's Cheryl, from next door," a woman replies, and Dancy chews at her lip, trying to think of the most reasonable excuse not to open the door. "If it's a bad time, I can come back later," says Cheryl. "I don't want to be a nuisance."

Dancy almost tells her yes, I'm sorry, it's a very bad time. But then she remembers the bottle of strange black pills and the watchful darkness pooled in the psychiatrist's eyes, and she slides the chain the rest of the way free, turns the latch for the deadbolt, and opens the door. She manages to force only the faintest sort of smile, but she figures that uninvited visitors can't be too picky about how they're greeted. The blonde from next door is holding a plate wrapped in aluminum foil, and she's smiling a smile that looks much more genuine than Dancy's.

"I made some cookies," she says. "I pretty much inevitably end up baking too many whenever I bake, so I thought you might like some. They're oatmeal, with raisins."

Dancy looks at the foil-wrapped plate, thinks how much she hates raisins, which have always reminded her of dead insects, and then she nods and says thank you and asks Cheryl if she would like to come inside?

"Sure," replies Cheryl. "But I can't stay long. I need to clean the kitchen before Joe (or Jo) gets home. I hate leaving the place a mess, but I wanted to bring these over while they're still warm." And she holds the plate out to Dancy, who takes it and steps aside so the woman can get past. Dancy shuts the door again, but doesn't lock it.

"I don't think anyone has ever brought me cookies," she says, and she tries to remember if that's really true or not.

"There's always a first time for everything, isn't there?" Cheryl asks her, glancing about the small room at the tawdry rented furniture and the dingy not-quite yellow walls, and a feeling of déjà vu hits Dancy hard enough that she almost drops the plate. "This is almost exactly like our place," the blonde says. "Only we get two windows, because we're on the corner. Would you believe we have to pay an extra fifty bucks a month for that damn window?"

Except for her p.o. and the exterminator and, once when the sink backed up, a plumber, this is the first time since Dancy moved in that anyone's been in the apartment with her. "Have a seat," she says, and she motions to the table and the two chairs at the table.

"I can't stay for long," Cheryl says again, but she goes to the table, pulls out the chair that Dancy usually sits in, and makes herself at home. "Joe will be home at six, and she hates when I leave a mess in the kitchen."

"She's your girlfriend?" Dancy asks, taking the seat across from Cheryl, the chair she never sits in. She glances at the prescription bottle, and for some reason she finds she's surprised that it's still there.

"Yeah," says Cheryl, still smiling. "Me and Joe, we've been together almost two years now. We used to live up in Jasper, but then she got a job in Birmingham, and, anyway, it's just easier to live here, you know. People in Jasper ain't exactly too keen about queer girls shacking up together."

"No," Dancy says, "I guess not," because she doesn't know what else to say. She thinks that Cheryl would be pretty if she didn't wear so much blush and mascara, plus eyeshadow that's almost the same shade of blue as the walls of the psychiatrist's office. Cheryl's nails are cut short, but they're polished a bright pearlescent pink, like the sort of bubble gum you might find inside an oyster shell. Dancy's momma would have called her trashy, even without knowing she's a lesbian.

"I was born and grew up there," says Cheryl. "I really liked Jasper, but it's just easier being here, you know? Home ain't always really home, if you know what I mean."

"Would you like something to drink?" Dancy asks her, rather than answer that question. "I have water and Buffalo Rock. But it's tap water."

"Jesus God, girl, you drink the water that comes out of these pipes?"

"Not much," Dancy replies. "Mostly, I just cook with it. And bathe in it."

"Well, of course you bathe in it," Cheryl says, glancing around the room again, and her eyes fall on the crucifix nailed up over the headboard. "Are you a Catholic?" she asks.

"I was raised Catholic," Dancy tells her.

"There's a Catholic Church in Jasper," says Cheryl. "Saint Cecilia's, but I was raised Baptist. Now I guess I'm not really anything at all. I can't even remember the last time I set foot inside a church." And then she asks, "You don't have anything stronger than tap water and ginger ale?"

Dancy shakes her head, and she says, "I'm an alcoholic. I don't keep beer or hard liquor around." She quickly adds, "Or wine," before Cheryl can ask.

"What do you do about the wine at communion?"

"I haven't taken communion in a long time," she says. "Not since I got sober. I quit smoking, too."

And Cheryl says, oh, I see, and she goes back to looking about the room, like she's making a mental inventory of everything in the apartment, and Dancy wonders if maybe she and Joe are thieves, too, but worse thieves than just shoplifters.

"You mind if we have some music?" she asks, pointing at the old transistor radio on the little table by the bed. "I get kinda antsy if it's too quiet."

"Sure," Dancy says, and she gets up and switches on the radio for Cheryl. There's a burst of static, and then Johnny Cash is singing the last verse of "Wayfaring Stranger." *She's not gonna like this,* Dancy thinks. *She's going to ask me to change the station to rock and roll or rap or something,* but Cheryl's busy staring out the open window and doesn't say anything about Johnny Cash.

Dancy's just sitting down again, when Cheryl says, "I heard you have a kid somewhere. But that you don't have custody, anymore. That you were in prison for a while after you kidnapped her. That her daddy had custody. Something like that. I don't recall all the details."

"Who told you that?" Dancy asks, and she can feel how her face has gone hot and flushed, and it feels almost like someone's just slapped her.

"I don't remember that, either. Might have been the super. Might have been those kids down on the first floor. Is it true?"

And Dancy's about to forget her manners and tell the woman that none of it's any of her business, that she doesn't care for gossips or people who repeat gossip, when Cheryl leans forward in her seat, leaning towards the window sill, and she asks, "Have you seen that mutt that's been hanging around? Big black son of a bitch. Joe keeps saying she's gonna call animal control, but she ain't yet."

"No," Dancy lies. "I haven't seen a dog around," and she tells herself that Cheryl didn't mean anything, that she wasn't trying to be mean, bringing up prison and Dancy's kid. Some people just don't know any better, that's all.

"Jesus God, it's a brute," says Cheryl. "A wonder it hasn't attacked anyone. And you just know the damn thing ain't had its rabies shot. I saw it last night, when I was going to bed, sitting right out there on the street, and I swear it was watching the building."

"I haven't seen it," Dancy tells her a second time. On the radio, "Wayfaring Stranger" ends and another song begins. It starts off with a rumbling clap of thunder and the sound of rain, like salt pork frying in a skillet, and then a man with a voice not so very different from the thunder or a tent-revival preacher drunk on whiskey and the Holy Spirit begins singing.

A'lookee yonder! A'lookee yonder!
A'lookee yonder! A big black cloud come!
A big black cloud come!
Yeah, come to Tupelo! Come to Tupelo!

"I heard this song in a bad dream," Dancy says out loud, not meaning to, but she says it aloud, anyway. It really doesn't matter, though, because Cheryl doesn't seem to be paying attention.

"Gave me the creeps, that dog sitting down there watching the building like that. Watching people while they sleep. Maybe I'll call animal control tonight. Summer's coming on, and dogs go mad in summertime. I suppose that's why it's called the dog-days."

And Dancy wants to say no, that's not why, because in high school she had a science teacher who told her it was because of the dog star, Sirius, which is in the constellation Canis Major, the big dog. "It's only a stray," she says, instead. "There are probably a lot of strays around here." She gets up and switches off the radio, then sits down on the edge of the bed, instead of going back sit at the table with Cheryl.

"But you just said you hadn't seen it?"

"Well, I don't know," Dancy says, feeling sick, feeling like maybe she's going to vomit, and she doesn't want anyone around when she does.

"Either you did or you didn't," Cheryl says, still staring out the window. "Either way, I'd be careful. It doesn't pay to talk to strangers, and that includes stray dogs who sit outside all night watching the building where you live."

Dancy shuts her eyes, trying to stop hearing the song from the radio, that evil fucking song about Tupelo and a killing flood of black rain and children being buried in shoeboxes tied shut with red ribbon. She's trying even harder not to think about the dog.

The dog is only a dream I have sometimes. Or only something I imagine I see when I'm off my meds. I know that now. Because dogs don't talk. Not to us. Not in English. Dogs don't follow people down the road singing hymns. Animals don't talk.

"What's her name?" Cheryl asks, and somehow the question forces Dancy to have to open her eyes again, and the first thing she sees is the prescription bottle of shiny black pills still waiting for her. Cheryl's looking at her now, instead of looking out the window.

"Whose name? What's whose name?"

"Your little girl's. What's her name?"

Dancy opens her mouth to tell her, but then she realizes she doesn't know. And how can that be? How can you forget your daughter's name? Not even the meth and the booze and all the shit that happened in jail, not even the pills that are supposed to keep her from seeing talking black dogs can make a woman forget her own child's name.

"You should go now," Dancy says, and the words come out harder than she means. They come out like someone throwing rocks. "I'm not well. I need to lie down for a while. I need to rest. I'm sorry."

"No, girl, that's fine," Cheryl says, and she's smiling again, smiling like she knows a secret the whole world would give its soul to learn, smiling like Dancy hasn't just said she feels sick. "Hope you enjoy the cookies. And you get some sleep, you hear? A good night's sleep will work wonders."

Cheryl lets herself out, and Dancy sits on the bed, trying to remember the name of the girl she gave birth to, the girl she took to Tupelo, but there's only the smell of kudzu, so strong and sweet it almost makes her gag.

6.

After the sun goes down, Dancy switches on every light in the apartment. She lies down on the bed, not bothering to turn back the blankets and sheets, just lying on top of the covers, and she stares up at the water stain on the ceiling. The radio is on, tuned to a news station, all news all the time, 24/7/365, so there's no possibility that she'll have to hear the song about Tupelo again. The announcers come and go, swapping voices, swapping genders, droning in confident, authoritarian tones about the rioting in Indonesia and President Clinton's reaction, about the failure of a communications satellite and how nobody's pagers are working, about how after forty-two years CBS won't be airing *The Wizard of Oz* anymore, so now it'll only show on cable.

For a while, Dancy can hear Cheryl and Joe (or Jo) through the wall, having a heated argument, but she can't make out many of the words, too few to know what they're fighting about. Afterwards, muffled only slightly by the plaster and lath, she can hear Cheryl crying. And after that, Mr. Watts turns his TV on loud enough that everyone in the place is probably getting an earful. Besides being drunk most of the time, he's more than half deaf. Dancy listens until his ballgame's over, until he goes to bed and down to whatever dreams winos who used to fight Japanese soldiers dream. The old wind-up alarm clock on the little table by the bed says it's eleven thirty-four. The building is mostly silent and still, except for the radio and the ticking clock and all the indistinct sounds that buildings make when the people who live in them are sleeping or lying awake, unable or unwilling to sleep. It's only a few blocks from the redbrick building to the Southside police precinct and Birmingham Fire Station 3, and so there are the occasional sirens to help the radio keep the silence at bay. Right now, Dancy doesn't want silence, any more than she wants the dark, any more than she wants to sleep.

After Cheryl left, Dancy sat down at the table by the window with a yellow legal notepad and a ballpoint pen, and she started listing all the names she could think of that anyone might give a girl baby. Probably, she even made up a few, and she was sure to include names that work for both boys and girls. But none of them jogged her memory. The list ran to more than three hundred and fifty names, and not a single one of them was one she recognized as the name of her laughter. Then, she tried another approach, writing down everything he *could* recall about the child, that she wasn't an albino, that her hair was auburn, that her eyes were hazel brown, that her favorite kind of sandwich was mayonnaise and pineapple. That she loved the Smurfs and Road Runner cartoons, and when she was four, she'd caught the measles and almost died. And though Dancy could clearly recall all of these things and much, much more, the name remained hopelessly out of reach, a blank spot in her mind that refused to be filled. Finally, she gave up and sat staring at the unlabeled prescription bottle and the black pills inside.

There's no reason you should be suffering, not if you don't have to suffer. No one has to hurt anymore.

Dancy tore out all the pages filled with baby names and threw them away, stuffed them deep into the trashcan beneath the kitchen sink and covered them over with other garbage. Then she took the prescription bottle to the bathroom, raised the toilet lid, and sat on the edge of the cast-iron, clawfoot tub, trying to find the courage to flush the black pills. The porcelain toilet bowl is a shade of green that usually reminds her of moss, but tonight it reminded her of Dr. Georgia James' eyes, before the darkness crawled inside the psychiatrist's skull. Dancy sat there on the tub until her butt began to go numb, trying desperately to believe that no one, not even someone who's a drug addict and a schizophrenic, is capable of forgetting her own daughter's name. After half an hour or so, as the day faded slowly to twilight, she left the bottle on the back of the toilet and went to bed.

Four hours later, and she hasn't even gotten up to pee.

Dancy knows that the dog is down there now, sitting on the sidewalk or in the parking lot, gazing patiently up at the building. She hasn't gone to the window to check, because she doesn't have to. She can *feel* it down there, watching, waiting, same as she can feel her own heart beating. She shuts her eyes and tells herself that in the morning she'll call the psychiatrist, and Dr. James will have an explanation.

Dr. James will even know her daughter's name, and just as soon a she says it, Dancy will remember it, too. The psychiatrist will say he forgetting was only a psychotic episode, a dissociative event, temporary amnesia, something like that. Everything the doctor says wil be convincing. Everything she says will seem absolutely reasonable Because, after all, isn't that the psychiatrist's greatest sin, the ability to make even the most absurd idea sound completely reasonable? Isn' that why she's been condemned to spend every weekday afternoor sitting in the blue room, in that nowhere in-between place, talking to crazy people?

If I had a gun, Dancy thinks, *I could kill the dog. If I had a gun I could at least frighten it away, scare it so bad it would stop hangin around here.*

Yeah? That day in Tupelo, you had a gun then, and it didn't frighter anyone you wanted it to frighten.

The alarm clock ticks, and the redbrick building that's stood here on the side of the mountain since 1916 makes its popping, creaking shifting, settling noises. Through the transistor radio, the newscasters rattle on endlessly, helping to keep the quiet at bay, telling Dancy what's happening out there in a wide, wide world that she'll never see. From far away, off towards downtown, comes the whistle and clatter of freight trains rolling on steel wheels and steel rails, rushing through the city on their way to somewhere else. The window's still open, and the room smells like kudzu. And Dancy lies on the mattress below the water stain, and sometime, not too long after midnight, despite her best intentions, she falls asleep.

7.

Dreaming, Dancy Flammarion travels sunbaked back roads and takes shelter from thunderstorms in abandoned churches, in usting railroad cars, and in farmhouses where maybe no one has lived since before the Great Depression. Always, she is trailed by a demon with four faces and a flaming sword, a demon or an angel (it hardly matters which) driving her ever forward, herding her from day to day, night to night, from one dank recess of nightmare to another. There is never any looking back, and there is certainly never any *going* back. She dreams a universe where there is no mercy, not even the scant mercy of remembering where she's come from, much less the knowledge of where she's going. Sometimes, she's hardly more than a child, the lunatic foot soldier of a vengeful God, her two hands for his red work, and other times she's an old, old woman who sits alone on the front porch of a tin-roofed shack at the edge of wide green fields of soybean and corn and sorghum, waiting for someone whose name she's forgotten to come home so that she can let go and die. The dream tumbles like dice in a gambler's sweaty palms, never lingering anywhere long enough that she can truly get her bearings.

The dice roll and the quicksilver architecture of the dreaming shifts again, and here it is a brilliant autumn morning, early October in Mississippi hill country, and she's been driving since sometime the day before, since she left Pensacola for the last time she'll ever have to leave Pensacola. A few hours more and she'll be in Memphis. There's someone waiting for her there in a rented room above a bar on Beale Street, the man whose car she's driving, the man who wired her the money for the trip, the smiling man with silver teeth and glass eyes who is the father of her daughter, the child riding in the back seat, singing to herself and watching the procession of red and yellow leaves and the wide carnivorous sky laid out above them. That sky has teeth, and Dancy has repeatedly cautioned the girl not to look at it too long nor too directly. A sky like that one, you should never, ever look directly at it, but only give it furtive, sidewise glances, same as you would a mean and angry dog.

The car radio is on, and a woman is singing "Wayfaring Stranger." The girl in the back seat is singing along, "I'm only going over Jordon I'm only going over home."

Dancy passes a green city limits sign, Welcome to Tupelo, All America City, We Let Our Hospitality Show, and now there's more than just the single straight line of Highway 78 pointing the path ahead. Now there are choices to be made, even if she chooses not to make them. There are shop fronts and convenience stores, churches, used car dealerships, fast-food restaurants and honkytonks and motels with soft beds and blue swimming pools that have been drained for the season and left to lay empty beneath the hungry sky. *If only this were as far as she had to go*, she thinks, *wouldn't that be marvelous?* If only she could stop here, instead of going on to Tennessee. If only Tupelo were her final destination, she could drive and find that the smiling man, who has promised three times now to make her his wife, has built them a beautiful house with tall stained-glass windows and a deep storm cellar and a swing set out back for the girl.

"This is where Elvis came from," she tells the girl. "You can still see the house where he was born. Would you like that? To see the place Elvis was born?"

Then Dancy glances at the dashboard, at the gas gauge, and sees that the needle is hovering just above empty, even though she could have sworn she filled the tank back in Tremont, right after she crossed the state line.

"We're gonna have to stop for gas, baby," she says, but the girl just shrugs and sings "Wayfaring Stranger" a little bit louder and watches the sunny world slip by outside the car window. "If you need to pee, you should do it here. Then maybe we won't have to stop again for a while." And anyway, Dancy hasn't fixed since back in Alabama, so now she can kill two or three birds with one stone. There's a rolled-up brown paper bag with a couple of syringes, a spoon, and enough crystal to see her comfortably to Memphis tucked beneath the front seat.

The gun's hidden under there, too, the Colt .38 and a box of shells, bought cheap out of the back of a pickup truck from a guy whose number she'd gotten from the smiling man. Dancy's grandfather taught her how to shoot when she was still just a kid, because he said everyone should be able to handle a gun, same as everyone should know good snakes from bad and how to swim. But she doesn't like guns, she doesn't like them at all. They make her nervous, and she's seen people shot, and she's seen people killed. She once saw a woman shot in the face, just because she said the wrong thing at the wrong time to the wrong person, saw the back of the woman's head come off and her brains sprayed across a wall. Still, the smiling man had insisted, even though she said she'd be just fine without one. *Nothing left to chance,* he told her. *You won't need it. Of course, you won't. But if you do, there it will be. You gotta be smart, and you gotta kill your fear, if you're gonna pull this off.*

She decides on a BP station up ahead, so she switches off the radio and tells the girl to hurry and put her sweater and her shoes back on, to be sure her laces are tied tight and to be careful not to knot them. She's six years old now, and that's plenty old enough to know how to tie your own shoes without getting the laces tangled in knots that your mother has to undo for you. The girl says she wants a Pepsi, and Dancy says sure, you can have a Pepsi, and she's wondering again how the tank could be empty, if she could possibly be mistaken about having bought gas in Tremont. If maybe she stopped, but got distracted and forgot to fill the tank. And then, just as she cuts the wheel right and the car bumps into the BP's parking lot, the dream shifts again, and Tupelo, Mississippi dissolves around her, melting into a hot summer night and a sky with more stars than she's ever seen before. If, indeed, Tupelo were ever truly there, if that day on the road and the child singing in the back seat, the gun and the drugs and her meth habit, if any of it were ever anything more than a scene from a movie she saw once on TV or from a paperback book she read. Maybe it wasn't anything but a bundle of unpleasant stray thoughts, her mind as tired as her feet and wandering off in place it ought not go, places she ought not *let* it go, making up stuff while she walks this narrow road between dead pine trees draped in a clinging death-shroud tangle of kudzu vines like a child's knotted laces.

Dancy's not at all sure how late it is, how late or how early depending on your point of view. If she had to make a guess, she'd say it's an hour or two after midnight, but not much more than that. She's been walking since sunset, walking at night to avoid the blistering white eye of the summer sun, that single unblinking eye of God that is so utterly unforgiving to her pale skin. Her right shoulder has finally stopped aching and gone numb from the weight of her duffel bag and the black umbrella tied onto it with a length of twine. She stops and lets the worn canvas bag slide off her shoulder and into the weeds and gravel at the side of the road. The night air is heavy with the rosin smell of the dead pines pressing in close on either side of the highway and with the sweet grape-jelly scent of kudzu blossoms. And even this long after dusk, there's also the odor of cooling asphalt, and she wonders if it's gonna be hard before morning, before the next day's heat comes along to melt it all over again.

She glances back the way she's come to see if the shaggy black dog's still following her. It is, still walking right down the middle of the road on its long legs like it thinks dogs never get run over by trucks and cars. If she stands here very long, it'll catch up with her again, and she doesn't want to talk to it anymore, doesn't want to hear the things it has to say. The last couple of miles, it's been singing hymns, mostly "Wayfaring Stranger," over and over and over again. Sometimes it gets all the words right, and sometimes it makes up its own words, and some other times it just hums.

It looks up at her, and its eyes flash blue-green iridescence.

"Ain't you getting tired yet?" the dog barks. "You aiming to keep on walking all the damn night long?"

"I walk until it's time to stop," she replies, and the dog snorts.

"Well, I think my paws are bleeding. At this rate, I'm gonna wear them straight on down to the bone and gristle."

"I don't remember anyone asking you to follow me. You can stop anytime you want. I wish you would."

"Why are you in such an all-fired hurry?" the dog asks, and then it makes a smacking, thirsty noise.

"Why are *you* following me?"

"I asked you first," the dog tells her, and then it trots the last few yards between them to the spot where the albino girl's standing and sits down in the weeds beside her duffel bag.

"That's my business. It ain't none of yours."

"La-dee-fucking-dah," barks the black dog.

The black dog is bigger than any dog she's ever seen before, bigger than the bloodhounds her granddaddy used to raise.

Back the way they've come, a pair of headlights appears, shining twin beams in the dark, and Dancy holds out a thumb. If she's lucky and the driver stops for her, she can get away from the talking dog. If she's really lucky, maybe the driver will be going to Bainbridge and she won't have to walk the rest of the way.

"That's not safe," the dog says.

"What's not safe?"

"Hitching like that. All sorts of degenerates and preverts out on a night like this. You won't catch me climbing in a car with strangers. Not for love nor money."

"Shut up, dog," she says, and then the car rushes past them without even slowing down. Dancy catches the briefest glimpse of the driver, a heavyset man with a bald head and beard.

"You best be glad he didn't stop," the dog tells her.

Dancy starts to reply, then realizes how bad the dog stinks. She wrinkles her nose and wonders if it's been rolling in something dead, if it found a road-kill armadillo or a possum or maybe even a whole dead deer. "You smell awful," she says.

"You're not exactly a bushel of roses your own self," the dog snaps back and flares its damp nostrils, sniffing the air around her. "When *was* the last time you made the acquaintance of a bar of soap?"

"At least I don't smell like rot," she tells the dog and rubs at her shoulder, which is getting the feeling back and has started aching again.

"Don't you fool yourself, girl. You *reek* of death."

"Dogs can't talk," Dancy says, hoping that will settle the matter once and for all. Then, just for a second, she remembers a conversation she once had with a woman she's never met, a woman who looks like she could be a librarian or a school teacher. Dancy remembers sitting with the woman in a room with blue walls, blue like empty motel swimming pools, and she said to the woman, "The dog is only a dream I have sometimes. Or only something I imagine I see when I'm off my meds. I know that now. Because dogs don't talk. Not to us. Not in English. Dogs don't follow people down the road singing hymns."

The woman smiled and told her, "Last summer, the first time you came to see me, you said the dog followed you all the time, everywhere you went, that it would never be quiet and leave you alone. You told me that the dog was the real reason you bought the gun. You remember that?"

A screech owl calls out in the woods somewhere very close by and the memory of the conversation in the blue room slips away from her. The owl cries out again, a mournful sort of cry like the whinny of a very small horse, a horse so small that fairies could ride it, if she believed in fairies and tiny fairy horses. There's a whippoorwill, too, but it sounds farther away even than the owl.

That woman was nothing ever happened, Dancy thinks. *I'm tired, that's all. I'm plumb wore out,* and she reaches for her duffel bag, the fraying canvas straps that have worn blisters and calluses on her back and both shoulders. "I can't stand around all night," she says to the dog. "I'm wasting time."

"And besides, dogs can't talk," the black dog reminds her and laughs. She's never heard a dog laugh before, and the sound makes the hairs on the back of her neck prick up and sends goose bumps up and down her bare arms.

"How about you leave me alone," she says, lifting the heavy bag, heaving it up onto her left shoulder. "Go home. Or are you some sort of stray?"

"That would mean we had something in common, wouldn't it, if I was a stray?"

"Shut up," she says and starts walking again. "And stop following me."

"You don't own this road," the dog barks at her.

"You stop, or I'll start throwing rocks at you."

The dog laughs again, and she can hear its feet on the pavement, the clicking of its long nails on the blacktop.

"I got myself some pretty sharp teeth," the dog says, "if I do say so myself. You probably ought to think twice about that before you start in chucking rocks. Anyhow, I've a pretty good notion where it is you're headed, and, tell you the truth, buttercup, I ain't so keen to meet up with that smiling man and his shiny glass eyeballs. If I were you, I'd think twice about all them pretty promises he's made you."

"Dog," she says, "I ain't got any idea what you're talking about," which, in this moment, on this night, is the truth.

"Sure you don't. But mark my words, you will soon enough," and then the dog clears its throat and goes back to singing.

"I am a poor wayfaring stranger,
Traveling through this world of below.
But there's no sickness, toil, or danger
In that bright world to which I go…"

Dancy stops and glares over her shoulder and the duffel bag at the dog. "Don't you know any other songs?" she asks it. "I'm sick to death of hearing that one."

"Oh, hell. I know lots of songs," the dog replies and licks its muzzle. "But this one's my favorite."

"Stop *following* me," she tells the dog again, and now she starts walking much faster than before, thinking that perhaps the dog's telling the truth and its paws really are sore, so if she walks fast enough it'll give up and leave her alone. But behind her, its claws are still clicking loudly against the road, and it's already started singing again.

> "I'm going there to see my mother
> She said she'd meet me when I come
> I'm only going over Jordan,
> I'm only going over home."

Dancy looks down at the road and the scuffed toes of her old boots, and because she doesn't know what else to do, she starts singing along with the black dog.

> "I know dark clouds will gather 'round me.
> I know my way is rough and steep.
> Yet beauteous fields lie just before me,
> Where God's redeemed their vigils keep."

And the sticky, warm south Georgia nighttime and the ebony ribbon of Highway 97 stretches out before her, all tar and perdition and possibility, leading the way east towards sunrise and all the terrible things that are waiting there for her, the things she knows and those she doesn't. Behind her, the big black dog begins the next verse of "Wayfaring Stranger," and the dreaming – restless, mercurial, possessed of no regard for narrative integrity – shifts again.

In a BP store on the outskirts of Tupelo, Dancy is waiting impatiently on the teenager running the cash register to stop talking on the phone and ring her up. Her head is buzzing like a swarm of yellow-jacket wasps, treading the meth's crackling euphoric haze, and she's having trouble standing still. She wants to be back on the road, behind the wheel and moving again, getting nearer and nearer to Memphis and farther and farther from Pensacola. She glances at the door, at her car sitting out there by the pumps, and then she looks back down at the counter and the seemingly random assortment of items she scrounged from the aisles and coolers – a handful of candy bars and two Diet Pepsis, a box of Band Aids, a bottle of water, beef jerky, a small bag of Cool Ranch Doritos, a box of Kleenex, and a quart bottle of motor oil. Finally, the boy gets off the phone, and she doesn't like the expression on his face, now that he's looking directly at her. He looks anxious, like something's about to happen any minute now and only he knows what that something is. And he looks as if he's afraid she'll reach across the counter and touch him, afraid whatever she is would rub off, and Dancy imagines the mantra running through his head, *filthy tweaker, albino freak, goddamn junkie weirdo.* "Is that all for you today, Ma'am?" he asks, and there's the slightest tremble in his voice. Dancy tries to tell herself there's nothing to it but the dope making her paranoid.

"A pack of Camel Lights," she says, sniffling, trying not to wipe at her nose or rub at her forearms, hidden beneath long sleeves. "And the gas. I'm on Pump Three."

"Yes, Ma'am," the boy says, and he turns to get the cigarettes.

He totals it all up, and Dancy pays him in cash.

"My daughter's still in the restroom," she tells the boy, and he nods, but now he isn't looking at Dancy anymore. Now he's looking out the plate-glass windows of the convenience store, instead, and anyone could see how scared he is. "Something the matter?" she asks him, her eyes following his, turning back towards the parking lot just in time to see the two dark blue Mississippi State Trooper cars pulling into the parking lot, no sirens, but the lights on the roof of the car flashing red and blue like Fourth of July fireworks.

"I don't want no trouble," the boy says. "This ain't got nothing to do with me, okay, and I don't want no trouble. Think about that little girl back there."

Dancy reaches for the pistol, tucked into the waistband of her jeans, hidden beneath her shirt, and the state troopers are getting out of their cars.

"Did you call them?" she asks, raising the shiny steel barrel of the Colt, pointing it at the boy. "*Look* at me, you son of a bitch! Did you fucking *call* them?!"

"Please, lady. Just think about your kid," he says again, and the gun in Dancy's hands feels almost heavy as an anvil, it feels like judgment on the last day of all, like the very word of Jehovah come down to smite the bloody battlefields of Armageddon, as Gog and Magog square off one last time. Only now the gun *isn't* a gun, at all. Now it's only a carving knife, and the morning sun glints dully off the blade.

In her dingy apartment in the redbrick building on the side of Red Mountain, Dancy opens her eyes, gasping awake like a drowning swimmer struggling to fill her lungs one last time before surrendering to the dark water of a flooded sand pit. Disoriented and sweat soaked, her chest aching and unable to get her breath, she's realizes that she's sitting in her chair at the table by the window. She remembers that she left all the lights burning, but they're off now. Every single one of them. The only light is coming from the streetlamps below. Her left hand is balled tightly into a fist, and when she opens it, she sees that she's holding the bottle of black pills that she left on the back of the toilet. Outside, down on the street, she hears a dog barking, only the barking sounds almost like words. Almost exactly like words.

Dogs don't talk. It's only a dream I have sometimes. Or it's only something I imagine I see when I go off my meds. I know that now, Dr. James.

Because dogs don't talk.

Dogs can't talk. Not to us.

And then the smell hits her, cloying and sweet as grape jelly, grape jelly and an odd fecund, spicy odor, the smell of growing things, a smell that is exactly what the color green would smell like, if colors had smells. Dancy stops staring at the pills in her hand and she looks up and sees what's happened to the apartment. It's filled wall to wall, floor to ceiling, with the vines and huge, fleshy heart-shaped leaves of kudzu plants. The furniture and the kitchen appliances have been reduced to nothing but indistinct shapes buried beneath the vines. There's no evidence whatsoever of the door. And as she lets the prescription bottle roll from her hand, Dancy sees a naked body huddled in a corner, *her* naked body wreathed in the vines like the trunks of smothered pine trees, like wooden power poles and abandoned boxcars. She can tell that the body isn't dead; it twitches like a sleeper lost in terrible dreams and desperately looking for a way out, like a little green anole lizard that's only almost dead. The vines have pushed their way inside her, getting in through her lips and nostrils and the two pits where her eyes used to be. Her pale legs are spread very slightly apart and a thick tangle of vines writhes there between her knees like a dying snake, thrashing side to side, burrowing, plowing, sowing seeds that will grow like glistening black pills. Her distended belly is as swollen as the belly of any pregnant woman.

Sitting at the table, watching as the kudzu monster changes her into something it can use, Dancy wants to scream. In all her life, she never wanted to scream even half so badly as she does right now. But she's afraid that if she makes any sound at all, the vines will notice that there's more than only the one of her. Then she hears something in the hallway and knows that it's the dog, even before it starts barking again, even before it rears up on its hind legs and begins scratching furiously at the apartment door hidden behind all those leaves.

There are lots of folks round here – and I mean the kind of folks it's best not to meddle with, best not to rile – who want to see you six feet under, 'cause of what you done. And what you're gonna do.

In a convenience store in Tupelo, a shimmering autumn morning is torn apart by gunfire and the sound of shattering glass and the terrified screams of a child whose name Dancy can't recall.

"I wouldn't want to be you," says the fat man behind the wheel of the Oldsmobile. "When it comes time to pay the fiddler, I sure as hell wouldn't want to be you."

Dogs can't talk. Not to us.

"That's horrible," the psychiatrist says, when Dancy has finished telling her about the dream of the kudzu in her apartment, the dream of the plants eating her alive. "I'm sorry. I really should have warned you. Nightmares have been reported as a rare side effect of this new medication."

Dancy only half listens while the psychiatrist talks. Here in the in-between place, neither sleeping nor awake, she sits in the wobbly chair with one leg that's too short and watches as the sun spills in warm through the window, through the open slats of the plastic Venetian blinds, and traces a lazy yellow-white path across the blue wall to her right. There is nothing about this room, she thinks, that has committed itself to being either one thing or another; it never takes a side. It doesn't have to. That's part of the deal. Everything here exists *between*. And though this place craves the dark, Dancy knows now that the sun, being an eye of God, can get in anytime it so desires.

"Dancy, are you listening?" the thing dressed up as a woman named Georgia James wants to know. "Did you hear me, or are you daydreaming?"

"I heard you," she says and looks down at her hands, at the empty prescription bottle she's holding. There's no label on the bottle, and it feels oily against her skin. "Which parts of it are a lie?" she asks. "That night on the road in Georgia and the talking dog? The fat man who stopped for me? My daughter? Tupelo?"

The psychiatrist sighs and frowns, and she sits up a little straighter in her chair. "You're only going to make this harder on yourself," she says. "There's nothing for you back there. There never was. Nothing but pain and suffering and disappointment, only people who want to hurt you for who and what you are, people who never loved you and who never will."

"Is *any* of it true?" Dancys asks, setting the empty pill bottle on the edge of the psychiatrist's desk. "Any of it at all?"

"It's nothing you haven't brought on yourself," replies the darkness in a voice like rustling kudzu leaves, the darkness peering out at her from its psychiatrist mask. "I want you to know that."

"Is my name even Dancy Flammarion?"

"There are rules," it tells her, ignoring the question. "There is a delicate balance, and you've upset that. These things you've done, the things you plan to do, you've shown absolutely no respect for the proper order of the world or your place in it, and it falls to me, I'm afraid, to see you don't make matters worse than you already have."

"My angel —" she says, but the darkness interrupts her.

"There *is* no angel, Dancy Flammarion. There is no talking dog. There is no wise fat man in a rusty car dispensing pearls of wisdom to grubby albino girls too stupid not to know their place in the skein."

Behind her, something's started scratching at the office door, and Dancy can feel the leaves and the fine prickling hairs on the kudzu vines brushing against her face and hands, against her throat and ankles, starting to slip in beneath her clothes.

"I ain't never been to Tupelo," she says, standing up, even though the vines are doing their best to hold her still. "I ain't never even been to Birmingham, for that matter. I don't have a daughter, and I can't remember her name because you forgot to *give* her a name."

The thing behind the desk has started shaking off the borrowed form of the psychiatrist, showing itself, and Dancy thinks it's like watching maggots squirming free of a corpse, thousands of wriggling black maggots. "You cannot even begin to imagine, child, what you've gotten yourself into. You'll never reach Bainbridge, much less Waycross or Savannah or any of those other places you've taken it into your foolish head to visit. Even if we don't stop you here, someone else surely will. You're nothing but a raggedy child, lost and alone."

Behind Dancy, the door to the in-between place splinters and comes apart, and the black dog hurls itself past her and over the desk, snarling and its lips curled back to show those sharp teeth it was telling her about. All around them, the blue room is unraveling, and Dancy sees that it's only another trick that's failing now that the darkness is too busy with the dog to keep the fragile illusion from collapsing into nothing more than a tunnel of vines and leaves. There's kudzu twined tightly about her wrists and ankles, and Dancy, still feeling more asleep than awake, sits staring at them until the dog growls her name.

"I can't very well fight this damn thing *and* drag your skinny white ass outta here," it barks, and then the darkness rises up above them, swelling and then crashing down again, engulfing and swallowing the dog whole. And, finally, that's enough to get her moving. Dancy rips at the vines, pulling herself free, crawling on hands and knees through the labyrinth of kudzu and rotting logs, past all the junk the kudzu patch has engulfed and covered over across all the years, the rotten bones of its meals crunching beneath her weight. Something wet and strong slithers out of the murk and wraps itself about her waist, trying to drag her back the way she's come. But Dancy kicks and tears at it and digs her fingers into soil and stone until she's hauled herself the last few inches and she's out beneath the stars again, scrambling through weeds towards the gravel ballast at the edge of Highway 97. She gets to her feet, her clothes torn and her legs a little unsteady, but in only a few more seconds she's standing on the far side of the road, looking back towards the vast sea of kudzu and dead trees. Somewhere in there, deep down in the shadows where starlight and the light from passing cars and trucks can never reach, the dog whimpers and falls silent. For another minute or two, the leaves rustle violently, but then they suddenly grow still, and she might only be looking at any kudzu patch on any back road.

That's its best trick of all, Dancy thinks, *laying right there in plain sight for everyone to see, but no one ever seeing it for what it really is.*

Dancy waits for the talking dog to come bounding back out of the kudzu, and then she sits down on her duffel bag, which she found lying in the weeds, and waits some more. But after awhile the sky begins to grow brighter as the stars fade and wink out one by one above the first violet-grey hints of dawn. And she knows that the dog's gone and gone for good, and she's alone again. She waits just a little longer, and then she picks up the heavy duffel bag and her black umbrella, ignoring the stinging red welts where the vines had hold of her.

"I'm sorry, dog," she says. "I should'a known better. I guess I do now."

And the albino girl named Dancy Flammarion spares one last glance at the kudzu patch, then turns and walks east towards the rising sun and whatever it is that happens next. And like the man says, Hell follows after.

TUPELO (1998)

This story was originally titled "The Last Temptation of Dancy Flammarion," and then it briefly became "St. Joan in Babylon." But it owes so much to Nick Cave and the Bad Seeds' song "Tupelo" that I finally just fucking gave up trying to pretend otherwise. As for the parenthetical date, 1998 refers not only to the year I first conceived of Dancy Flammarion but also to the year that *Threshold* is set (even though this story, as I explain in the afterword, is not part of that novel's continuity). As for its genesis, way back on January 8th, 2006, shortly after I'd finished "Bainbridge" for *Alabaster,* I wrote in my online journal:

Someday, in a moment of terrible weakness, I'll write a story wherein Dancy sidesteps her fate and has a long life entirely devoid of monsters. It would be a lie, but I might find comfort in it, anyway.

When the story that would become "Tupelo (1998)" first occurred to me, in December 2016, it was going to *be* that story. I needed to write something hopeful, no matter how delusional that happiness might be. I began work on it the next month, and originally the text began with this paragraph:

Sometime in the night, the cold rain began to freeze, and by dawn the storm had transformed all the world into a scene from a Christmas card. The sort of winter scene that's accentuated with patches of silver and white glitter glued here and there to make it seem more like you're looking at the real thing. And when you handle the card, no matter how carefully you handle it, some of the glitter always, inevitably rubs off and sticks to your hands and your clothes. This is how it seems to Dancy, standing at the bedroom window, looking out across the backyard towards the pines and poplars and dogwoods that mark the edge of the yard and the beginning of the forest.

Anyway, I quickly realized that the hopeful, merciful story I'd *wanted* to write in December, that one in which Dancy has a normal life and never has to fight monsters, wasn't something I *could* write just then. In fact, it might be a story I should *never* write. Perhaps it was even actually a story I don't know *how* to write.

Those do exist, you know.

I will also add that there are an *awful* lot of autobiographical details in this one.

And that "Tupelo (1998)" is the longest of all the Dancy stories.

Dreams of a Poor Wayfaring Stranger

1.

Behind her is all the fire that ever was, the righteous heaven-spun fire of the seraph that has burned down her life and scorched the summer sky white as bleached bones and melts the highway beneath Dancy Flammarion's feet. The asphalt may as well be no more than licorice left too long in the sun, the way it sticks to the soles of her boots and slows her down, holds her back, a vast stripe of licorice and tar to divide the pines and the kudzu and the South Alabama day so that she cannot ever get lost in this wilderness and wander without even knowing her left from her right. She would look back over her shoulder at the firestorm, but she knows too well that it would blind her. It would burn the eyes from her skull and damn her to darkness for however long she has left to live. In *this* dream, it would do exactly that, no matter how many times her *waking* eyes have looked into that selfsame inferno with no more protection than a pair of shoplifted sunglasses and been left nothing worse than dazzled and aching. The day roars with the fire, and the sky crackles with it, and the very ground beneath her feet shudders as all the land behind her is washed in those merciless flames, as the day burns and burns and burns but never is consumed. Black vultures wheel above her, and crows, too. There are dead things all along the highway, the roadkill carcasses of possums and armadillos and coyotes, raccoons and deer, and she is very careful to step over or around all these broken, rotting bodies. The day simmers with the stench of decay and brimstone and melted pitch, and Dancy wishes that the scalloped shadow cast by her tattered black umbrella were a little more substantial. She wishes also there were a dark culvert somewhere nearby that she could climb down to and huddle inside until nightfall comes round again, concrete shadows that are not cool – because there is no genuine coolness left in this land, because the seraph has seen to that – but shadows that even stifling would still *seem* cool by comparison. There might also be a kindly trickle of creek water running through the culvert, and even warm it would seem like ice against her cracked lips and parched tongue. Sweat streaks her face and drips to the asphalt and sizzles and boils away to steam in an instant.

Maybe this time you have marched me straight into Hell, she thinks. *Maybe that's where we've been headed all along.*

"No," says the pretty woman walking along beside her. "This ain't Hell. It's only an August day. It's only an August in Covington County. I expect you'll know Hell when you see it."

"*How* will I know?" Dancy asks her.

"You'll know," the pretty woman tells her.

The woman is pale, but not half so pale as Dancy Flammarion, and her eyes are filled up with the seraph's roiling fire, and her hair is the color of straw. She's wearing a blue calico dress speckled with tiny yellow flowers. She isn't wearing any shoes.

"How can you walk barefoot on this hot road?" Dancy asks her. "It's hot as a skillet. Probably it's hotter than that."

The pretty woman shrugs and looks down at her feet. "I don't suppose I've stopped to think about it," she says. "I suppose my mind's been chewing on too many other things."

"Like what?"

But instead of answering the question, the pretty woman with straw-colored hair starts in talking about priests and monks and shamans who can walk unharmed across hot coals or stones, ash and cinders. Dancy starts to say something about how all those firewalking people are heathens and how heathens get away with all sorts of things righteous, god-fearing folks can't, but, before she has the chance, the woman says, "You're hard, Dancy. You're harder than you have to be. Sometimes, I fear you've let this angel's heat burn away your soul. You believe there's only one sort of good in all the wide world, and you know what that good is, and you can never be told any different. Not by me, not by anyone."

"I startin' to think maybe you're something evil," Dancy replies, and she walks a little faster now, and her heart beats a little faster. "I think maybe you're something awful I shouldn't be listening to or talking with or walking down this road beside."

"I *am* something awful," the woman tells her, "but then, so are you. We might almost be sisters, that way."

Behind them the seraph swings its burning sword and all its several faces howl in unison and its wings batter air.

"You have its fire inside you," says Dancy, pointing at the woman's eyes.

"Like I said, we might almost be sisters."

Or it's only a trick, and she's trying to fool me.

"I shouldn't be talking to you," Dancy says again.

"You seemed lonely, that's all. I hate to see anything as lonely as you looked. Anyway, you won't even remember me when you wake up. You'll forget all about me, and there will only be you and the angel again."

Dancy stops walking and unshoulders the heavy duffel bag, letting it fall to the sticky, melted-licorice road. She frowns and stares up at the white sky and the empty hole where the sun should be, but isn't.

"It ain't fair," she says, "following me in my dreams. I should be safe here. I should be safe here, even if I can't be safe nowhere else."

"Who told you that?" the pretty woman asks her.

"No one," says Dancy. "I just think that's the way it ought to be."

"Well, it isn't," the woman says. "There are few places more dangerous than dreams, and if that angel back there really cared about you, it would have told you that a long, long time ago. No place is more dangerous than dreams, because in our dreams all our truest selves are laid bare. There aren't any masks in dreams, and there aren't any lies, either. There's nothing at all standing between *you* and *you*. I should have thought the angel would have told you that by now."

"You think you know an awful lot," Dancy says.

"Not so much," the woman tells her, "but I do know that."

"Well, okay, but I can't stand here talking all day. I'm supposed to be somewhere soon. I don't know where yet, but I *will* know, when I get there. So I can't stand here jabbering all day with you about dreams and heathens who walk on fire. Anyway, like I said, I'm kinda sure you're not something I should be talking with. I bet you got better places to be, too, so why don't you go off to one of those, instead of bothering me."

When the pretty woman doesn't reply, Dancy stops staring at the sky and realizes that she's alone again, alone except for the roaring seraph and the blistering summer day and all the dead things on the road and all the hungry black birds wheeling overhead.

2.

"What if they ain't bitin' tonight?" Dancy asks Mr. Jube, and the old man, old before she was born, he looks up at the full buck moon, just now clearing the tops of cypress trees girding the blackwater lake no one has ever bothered to name. He rubs his chin, then shuts his left eye, then opens it and shuts his right. He sighs, and all time and all the night seem echoed in that sigh. Dancy imagines it's the way that rocks would sigh, if they could. It's the way that very old trees might sigh.

"Well, I reckon if they ain't, they ain't. If they ain't, I'll have something besides catfish for my dinner, and I've had worse tribulations to contend with."

In this dream that she does not *know* is a dream, Dancy Flammarion is not yet the girl she will become; neither is she still the child she was. But Mr. Earl Jube is exactly the same as he has always been, as she has pressed him between her memories like dried flower petals, the descendant of men and women stolen from the Windward Coast of Africa, from Gambia and Senegal, and sold to Southern plantations. The great-great-grandson of slaves, and who in his youth had wanted to see great cities and so had traveled as far away as New York and Chicago before coming back to live in the little shack in Shrove Wood, the same little shack where he'd been born in 1912, the same year as Dancy's own grandmother.

In this dream that Dancy does not know is a dream, she's gone out with Mr. Jube in his leaky pirogue, all the way out to the very middle of the blackwater lake at the edge of Shrove Wood, the lake that swallows whatever flows down from Wampee Creek, and she sits on an upturned produce crate and watches while the old man baits his hook with bits of bread rolled between his fingers into tight little balls. He drops his line over the side and the lead weight carries it down to the muddy bottom. Then Mr. Jube switches off his flashlight, so there's only the glow of the moon. All around them, the night thrums with the songs of bullfrogs and cicadas, night birds and crickets. Every now and then, the throaty bellow of a bull alligator rolls across the water.

Dancy squints into the darkness, waiting for her eyes to adjust.

"You ever think about all the things must be down there?" Dancy asks Mr. Jube, and she points at the water. "Way down at the bottom of the lake, I mean."

"Besides muck and slime and fish shit?"

"Yeah, I mean besides that."

"I reckon there's some things it's just best we not think on too hard," he says. "Things maybe we're just better off not knowin' about."

"That ain't much of an answer," she says.

"No, I don't guess it is at that," says Mr. Jube, and then he takes a handkerchief from the bib pocket of his overalls and blows his nose.

"I think I'm old enough now to be askin' these sorts of questions," she tells him.

Mr. Jube puts his handkerchief away again, and he looks back over his shoulder at Dancy, then back at the place where his line disappears beneath the surface of the lake.

"That don't mean I'm old enough to be answerin' them," he says.

"What's that supposed to mean?" Dancy wants to know, and she dips the fingers of her right hand into the water. It's a lot colder than she expected.

"This lake, it's done been here a long, long time, and I reckon it ain't quite as full up with secrets as the sky or the seven seas, but also I reckon it's got its fair share. And more often than not, girl, secrets are secrets for a reason. More often than not, they're better off stayin' that way. And I also wouldn't go wagglin' my digits over the side like that, 'less you fancy some hungry gator or snappin' turtle coming along and bitin' them off."

"I swim in this water, and ain't nothin' bit me yet."

"Not at half past midnight on a full moon you don't," says Mr. Jube. "Not plum out in the middle of the lake like we are."

And because he has a point, she takes her fingers out of the water. But it's left something thick and oily on her skin, something that glistens iridescent in the moonlight like slug trails or mother-of-pearl.

Mr. Jube looks at her hand and frowns. "See now? That's exactly the sort of thing I'm talkin' about."

Dancy sniffs at her hand, then wipes it on her jeans.

"You think there are monsters in the lake?" she asks him. "Momma says there are. Momma says any lake where you can't see the bottom is bound to have monsters."

Mr. Jube gives his fishing pole a couple of gentle tugs, then looks up at the yellow-white moon and says, "Well, I figure there's plenty enough things wriggling around down there might as well *be* monsters. Whether or not we call 'em somethin' else don't much matter. I once saw a channel cat pulled outta this very lake every bit big enough to eat you whole without chewin'. This other time, I seen garfish long as a Ford pickup truck."

"But those are just big fish," says Dancy. "They're not real monsters."

"Don't the Good Book says it was a big fish swallowed Jonah, and what you reckon is more like a monster than that?"

"Things," says Dancy. "Worse things than that."

"Let me see you spend some time in a catfish's belly and then you tell me if you don't decide that's worse enough."

"I had a dream last night," she says. "Last night I dreamed we'd go fishin' tonight, and that you wouldn't catch nothin', and that we'd see a fallin' star over the lake, only it wouldn't really be a fallin' star. It would really be an angel come all the way down here lookin' for me. It had six wings and four faces and a burning sword, and it had come to take me off somewhere."

"Where pray tell would that be?" asks Mr. Jube and cocks an eyebrow, "where it was gonna take you off to like that?"

"I don't know. It didn't tell me. I didn't dream that part."

Mr. Jube shakes his head and sighs and clicks his tongue against the roof of his mouth. "Monsters," he says, "and angels with six wings and flamin' swords. You sure have got yourself a dark turn of mind, girl. I *will* give you that."

Dancy starts to tell him something the angel *did* tell her, something about werewolves and a caged panther and a rotten old house full of crazy women who eat people, but then she decides it's best to be quiet a while and watch the sky, instead.

Just in case.

3.

In popcorn-and-cigarette scented darkness, Dancy Flammarion sits beside the woman who may or may not be her mother, and the projector clicks and whirs and throws garish light and shadow onto the screen. Dancy cannot remember the name of the theater – the Bijou, the Roxy, the Odeum, the Fox, one of those or something else altogether – and she also cannot recall the name of the movie she's watching, though it must have been spelled out plainly enough on the theater's marquee. She must surely have looked up and seen it before she even stepped up to the box office and got her ticket, even if she hadn't known it before she set out on foot from the cabin on Eleanore Road. She at least half remembers doing that much, walking alone near twilight down Eleanore Road to the place it meets up with State Road 4 that would lead her on to the Milligan city limits. But Dancy remembers walking the road alone, not with her mother. Still, the woman in the seat on her right looks very much like her mother, Judith Flammarion, who might or might not have run away to Pensacola and almost drowned herself in the Gulf of Mexico the year before Dancy was born.

If it's her, I would know, thinks Dancy. *You don't go and forget the face of your own momma. You don't do a thing like that.*

Don't stare. It's rude to stare. It's cruel to stare and point and whisper.

So Dancy keeps her eyes on the screen, instead.

A moment ago, it was only black-and-white cowboys and Indians up there, horses and guns and bows and arrows, a cavalry bugle, a war cry, but now it's something else entirely. Now, all in Technicolor, the projector paints a flickering ghost town, someplace even smaller and shabbier than Milligan, someplace in the swampy low country that seems to have suffered a strange calamity, one that has left it entirely empty of people, that has left the windows of storefronts and of a drugstore and a gas station all shattered, the sidewalks and streets littered with glass like half a million broken diamonds. Dancy pretends to herself there's nothing at all familiar about the town, that she's never dreamed of it before. She thinks how she should just get up from her seat and leave the theater. Suddenly, she isn't in the mood for a movie anymore, and certainly not a movie she cannot even be bothered to remember the name of. She isn't in the mood to have to pretend she doesn't know what's happened to that town on the screen. Or to sit wondering whether the woman beside her is her mother.

On the theater screen, Dancy wanders the streets of the deserted, broken town, which she knows she's never done, but there it is happening, anyway. She comes to what once was a Greyhound bus stop, a lone park bench outside a boarded-up Esso station, and she sets down and starts waiting for a bus that isn't ever coming.

"It isn't only what you remember," says the woman on Dancy's right, speaking with Judith Flammarion's voice. "It's what you can't remember, too."

"I've seen a terrible lot of things weren't what they made themselves out to be," says Dancy, not taking her eyes off the screen.

"I know," says the woman with her mother's face and voice.

"Just because you look like her and sound like her, well, I've seen enough to figure that don't necessarily mean you *are* her."

"What if I can tell you things that only she would be able to tell you?"

"Like what?"

"Like the time your granddaddy brought home a box of tangerines called Dancys, and how you wouldn't believe I hadn't named you after a tangerine. Like that, for example. Or like the strawberry mark in the small of your back."

On screen, a red-winged blackbird lights on the back of the bench and starts talking to that make-believe Dancy, like just everyone in the world could talk to birds.

"Maybe you can read my mind," says Dancy. "Maybe you can see my thoughts just as easy as I can see this here movie."

The woman sighs and glances down at the green bag of popcorn in her hands. "Or maybe," she says, "this night is before you left. Maybe this night is before the fire and before I died, and so maybe we got another chance for it all to happen some other way round than how it did."

"My angel says I gotta be careful of seeing pretty things I want to be true and folks sayin' they want to help me, 'cause even if they come wearin' sheep's wool, inwardly they're ravenous as wolves."

"Or werewolves," says the woman. "Have you ever let yourself consider maybe your angel ain't no angel at all? That possibly it's something else? Something worse?"

Up on the movie screen, the movie blackbird knows just exactly who the movie Dancy is, and it knows the deeds she's done, all the evil she's cut down and the ground she's purified with blood and fire and just that once a bullet.

"But even so," squawks the bird, "even if all that's the undeniable gospel truth and not just spook stories monsters tell to other monsters, you ain't safe here. If that angel of yours got the sense god gave a hop toad, it'll tell you to leave this place."

"I never talked to that bird," says Dancy, turning towards the woman who might be her mother, the woman with her mother's voice and face.

"It's just a movie."

"Well, I never did."

"I didn't say any different, now did I?"

"This one time, up near Waycross, I talked with a red-wing blackbird, but it wasn't *that* bird there."

"Okay, fine, but the blackbird in Waycross, the one you *did* talk to, didn't it also try to warn you? Didn't it also try to tell you how just possibly you were bitin' off more than you could chew?"

"See, my momma wouldn't know that," Dancy tells the woman. "That didn't happen till after she died, so if you *was* her, then you wouldn't know nothin' about the blackbird in Waycross or what all it said to me."

"Fine. Have it your own way. You always were a pigheaded child. Anyhow, you're missin' the movie. Since you looked away from the screen, a lot's happened."

"I don't care about the movie. I don't want to see it. I don't even remember buyin' a ticket or what it's called."

"Wolves," the woman tells her. "Something about wolves, I think."

"Well, I still don't care."

The woman sighs again and again she looks down at her bag of popcorn.

"I was worried about you is all," she says. "I missed you, and I was worried, and I wanted to see how you were gettin' along. I didn't mean to upset you."

"I ain't upset," says Dancy, thought she knows that's a bald-faced lie. "I just don't want to be here is all. I don't want to see this movie, and I don't want to talk with whoever or whatever you are that ain't my momma."

"Then you ought'a reach for that knife of yours," the woman says, "or if you're not in the mood for killin' tonight, just wake up and forget we ever talked."

And Dancy Flammarion *does* start to reach for the butcher knife tucked into her left boot, but then she realizes that it isn't there, that she left it in the cabin, beneath her bed, before setting out for town. And that was stupid, stupid as stupid gets, but it can't be helped now. So she turns back to the screen, and discovers that it's only cowboys and Indians again.

4.

A black pit, or only a basement or root cellar so deep and dark it may as well be called a pit. So, a pit, and in the pit two cages hang suspended in the darkness, suspended like twin pendulums from rough-hewn pine timbers, but unlike pendulums hanging always perfectly still. Crudely built, squarish cages of wrought iron and some carved wood, the bars fashioned from razor wire and barbed wire and from bone, *human* bone, ribs and long bones wired together, and you do not dare touch one of those with bare skin, they're so sharp and, besides, electrified, same as a fence meant to keep in horses and cows or keep out deer. It doesn't matter that Dancy knows she's only dreaming that she's locked up inside one of the two cages, naked and curled fetal and listening to the darkness and the squeak of rats and the creak of the chains that hold the cages suspended in the pit. It doesn't matter, because whoever it was first said *only dreaming* was a fool and was so much a fool that you have to wonder if he or she had ever dreamed at all. Knowing the dream is a dream does not lessen Dancy's horror or pain, her hunger or thirst or fear. And she thinks, *What if I should happen to die in my sleep? Would I stay here forever? Would the dream just go on and on and on and on, what I get for telling the angel I was too tired to walk any more, so I was gonna sleep whether it said I could sleep or not?* In the other cage, the other naked girl whimpers, the dream girl whose name is Genesis, just like the first book of the Bible, and when Dancy asked her why anyone would name her daughter Genesis, the answer was, "My father named me, not my mother, and there are plenty of people named Daniel and Matthew and Mark and even Ezekiel, aren't there?" Dancy replied that wasn't at all the same, since all those names were names to start with, and the girl told her anyway, no one ever called her Genesis. "Well what do they call you then?" And the girl replied, "What difference does it make, now?" In this dream, the girl is missing both her egs below the knees and one arm below the elbow, amputated by the thing that built the cages, the thing that keeps them in the pit, the thing that has no name but wears an almost human face. The thing that is always hungry, but only rarely allows itself a treat from the cages hanging in the pit. So far, it has not cut Dancy. It says it's saving her for Thanksgiving or Christmas or some other Red Letter Day, but Dancy thinks the truth is that the thing is afraid to cut her. It wasn't too afraid to catch her and lock her up in this cage, but drawing her blood and roasting and eating her flesh, that might be another matter, entirely. In the other cage, the other girl whimpers again. "You go on back to sleep," says Dancy. "Go back to sleep and dream how we ain't here, how we ain't never been here or even had nightmares about any such place. Go back to sleep now." The girl doesn't answer, but she also doesn't whimper again, so maybe she's taken Dancy's advice. Maybe in this dream Dancy is a sort of hypnotist for dying girls locked in cages in root cellars, waiting to be sliced up and eaten and shat out again. She closes her eyes, trying not to hear the song the thing sings whenever it comes down into the cellar or the basement, this black pit that stinks of bare earth and worms and infection and little white mushrooms. She tries to shut it out, but she hears it, anyway, ringing about her skull. *O, what land is the Land of Dreams? What are its mountains, and what are its streams? O Father, I saw my mother there, Among the lilies by waters fair.* And Dancy opens her eyes again, and she thinks, *Let me wake up now, and I won't go to sleep except when you say that I can. I promise. I swear. Cross my heart.* Then something rustles in the darkness, and she realizes that she isn't alone, that the thing has crept down into the pit when she was busy telling the other girl to go to sleep or when she was busy trying not to remember the singing or to get the angel to let her wake up. She opens her eyes and there's a pool of candlelight, and there's the thing's almost human face, its almost woman's face, watching her, and it smiles. "When I was a child," it says, "I had a snake, and I fed it tiny white mice with twitching noses and pink eyes." The thing's voice makes Dancy think of the silence and the stillness before a tornado. "I'm not scared of you," Dancy says, but the thing ignores her and goes on with its story about being a child with an imprisoned snake. "I would drop them into its tank, hold them by their tails and drop them in, and I would watch when it coiled itself about them and squeezed out all the life and then swallowed them down headfirst." "You should let me out," says Dancy. "Now, why exactly is that?" asks the thing with the candle, and it takes a step nearer the cages. "You let me out," says Dancy, "and maybe my angel might let you live. Maybe I got more important places to be, and maybe my angel would tell me this was all a misunderstandin' and I should let you go on about your business and I should go on about mine." The thing silently watches her for a time, and its eyes are almost black as the blackness trapped inside the root cellar and it chews impatiently at its lower lip. "And what about her?" it asks, finally, and with the candle gestures towards the other cage and the other girl. "What about her?" Dancy replies. And the thing asks, "Would you *leave* her, *abandon* her, let me *keep* her for my own, for however much longer she might last?" In the dream, Dancy hesitates a moment, but only a moment, and then she says, "She ain't none of my concern. You do whatever you want with her. What's she to me, anyhow, just some girl who lies about her name, so you let me go, and you won't never see me again." The thing stops watching Dancy. Now it's watching the other cage, instead. "She's been here with me a long time," it says. "Lots longer than you. She fell asleep one night in her bed in her house in a city far away, and then she woke up here. She's lasted longer than any of the others ever did. I'm learning. I'm learning to be careful with the little white mice. I'm learning not to squeeze too hard all at once." *Please let me wake up now. Please let this dream be done with and let me wake up, and I won't ever disobey you ever again, and I'll walk from now until the Crack of Doom, if that's what you ask of me.* "I promise," Dancy says aloud, to her angel or o the thing with the candle or to both. "I'll be back later," says the thing. "I have company tonight, come a great distance to set eyes on ou, thinks maybe you're something special, something more than a little white mouse sent to keep me from starving. But I do hope she's wrong. I do so hope she lets me keep you for my own." And then he thing that only almost looks like a woman turns away from the cages, back towards the steep wooden stairs leading up to the world of sunlight and moonlight, and as it goes it sings, *Dear child, I also by pleasant streams have wandered all night in the Land of Dreams. But though calm and warm the waters wide, I could not get to the other side.*

5.

Opening her hand and closing it again on damp clay and soil and wriggling worms, and opening her eyes, and closing them again, opening them to moonrise, closing them to sunset, feeling the cool soil and clay blanket to keep her safe in the day and to release her at night, and dreaming always red dreams. Sleeping beneath the ruins of he old Baptist church by the river, and the others sleeping safe around her, and this is how Dancy Flammarion has come to understand that she has been lonely all her short life, that even the company of her mother and grandmother and grandfather were a sort of loneliness, a borrowed, secondhand loneliness because her family were all three of them lonely people, and so Dancy inherited their loneliness just as she inherited the gene for albinism and every other damn *and* damned hing. But then one night the hungry folk found her alone and lonely on the highway, somewhere halfway between Eleanore Road – which once had been what passed for home – and all the many sour, sun-scorched places that she had been charged with the going to and all he transgressors she'd been charged with the final judgment and exe-cution of, and the hard man with silver eyes had kissed her throat and promised that there was finally and forever an end to the loneliness. He kissed her throat, and he tasted her and said, "You're never gonna have to hear that bitch again," meaning the angel. All it took was a mouthful from his wrist, and the angel fell silent, or Dancy was struck deaf to its eternal howling, and either way the same merciful result. Either way release. Either way heaven after all she'd been through and done and had been told was still waiting to be done. And the hard man with silver eyes and all his children took her back to the ruined church with him to sleep away the hateful South Georgia days and to wake to the gentle, kudzu-scented nights, and to drink her fill and never, ever be hungry again. *You can leave,* he told her, speaking in that way he had of speaking without his lips ever moving. *If it turns out that's what you want. Any time you choose. No one will stand in your way. You are free now, for the first time ever, I'd wager, you're free.* That part she hadn't dared to believe, not at first, and she'd thought surely if she tried to go his voice would be there in her head or his blood in her veins like a magnet drawing her back to him. But then she left one night, and she was on her own for a month or more, and never once did she feel any tug or pull or tidal drag until she realized that she was lonely again, hunting all on her own, no one to share the red dream with, no one to talk to or sing to or listen to, and so she went back to the ruined church and the others. And now, imagining she is awake, she rises with the others and they walk the dark roads not so far from Bainbridge, where, she has been told, far worse things than them sleep the days away, and which place, says the hard man with silver eyes, she would do well to always, always, always give a wide berth. Tonight, the moon is almost full again, and they find a convenience store on the edge of town, and in they go, single file, the door swinging open with a cowbell jingle and jingling closed again behind the last of them. Behind the counter, a kid in a navy blue vest he's paid to wear, just as he's paid to stand behind that counter on this dark and lonely road all night, every night, and never mind who or what might come walking through the door. "Let me know," he says, "if I can help you." Dancy is the first to look at him, even before the hard man with silver eyes. She turns her head and smiles, not even trying to hide her teeth, and the boy doesn't smile back, but then she hadn't expected he would. No one ever smiles back. The kid says, "Hey, I don't want to trouble," and all the others are busy wandering the aisles, pretending they have any need or desire for candy bars or Pepsi Cola or Frito's brand corn chips. "No trouble," Dancy whispers, in that voice she has not yet been dead so long that it doesn't still take her by surprise every time she speaks. The kid's name is printed on a plastic badge and pinned to his vest. "Don't it get lonesome in here, Mason? Ain't this the most lonesome sort'a job in the whole world, bein' stuck in this dump all night by yourself?" And he shrugs his thin shoulders and looks down at the Formica counter and she can smell his fear like hot tar and vinegar. "It ain't so bad," he says. "I've done worse." But now there is a tremble in his voice, because now he has become, even if he's too dumb to know it, a small, small animal hunkered down in the brush and trying not to shiver and show its fear, waiting for something hungry, something with razor teeth and razor claws and silver, ball-bearing eyes, to pass him by and go eat someone else. "Ain't we all," says Dancy, and now the hard man has turned to watch her. Beneath the bright fluorescent bulbs, Dancy is a creature so perfectly pale as to seem almost spun from glass, all but crystalline in her perfection, a life form based not in dull carbon but silica, and if she isn't careful, she'll blind the boy before the fun's even begun. Don't be selfish, the hard man whispers behind her eyes. Remember, child, that we all of us have our appetites and this one ain't for you and you alone. And she says, "I know," and she says it aloud, and the kid behind the counter winces at the sound of her surprising, crystalline voice. "I won't make a pig of myself," she says. *Good,* the hard man whispers. *Good.* So, here's the kid behind his counter and his cash register, surrounded by a hundred useless fucking things – cigarettes

and condoms and dirty magazines, bubblegum and Made in China
novelty key chains and breath mints and Skittles in every color ever
was – and here's Dancy rendered whole by the kiss of the hard man
and sent out into the world and into the night and finally into this
convenience store to dream the red dreams. Here are the two of them,
the rabbit and the fox, the fat cottonmouth moccasin and the careless
bullfrog, and she takes a step nearer the counter. "I gotta gun," says
the kid, and Dancy, she says, "Oh, I know. But that's okay. You won't
need it, not tonight. But it's good that you have it, all the same. We all
gotta watch out for ourselves, way the world is these days. We all gotta
take precautions. How old are you?" And the hard man with the silver
eyes, he tells Dancy to be careful, that the kid's not bluffing and there
is a gun beneath the counter, a loaded Winchester shotgun, and it
might not kill her, but then again, it might. "I ain't foolin'," says the
kid. "I gotta gun. There ain't enough money in the register to bother
with, and I can't open the safe." And Dancy tells him that's okay, too,
that they don't want money, that they don't need money, not any
more, and the hard man – who has existed so awfully long and seen
so much that he is hardly ever amazed at anything these days – even
he is taken aback by the terrible beauty of what Dancy Flammarion
has become, her white hair like strands of starlight, her eyes like pools
of mercury, her voice so ruthless it might almost shatter diamonds to
dust, but so gentle, too, that it would lull a rabid dog down to the
sweetest, most peaceful red dreams all its own. So, you see, what
chance has this kid got? This skinny, terrified kid who has not yet
lived long enough to see his seventeenth year and not yet traveled far
enough from Decatur County to bother bragging about it and who
has not yet even lost his cherry, *this* kid was good as done for all along.
"You don't need that gun," says Dancy. "It'll be quick. It won't even
hurt." The lies roll off her tongue so easy and ring so fine and true
that even the hard man wants to believe them. And so does the kid, if
only because believing anything the opposite will only make matters

worse, and he isn't quite *so* stupid that he doesn't know by now he's drawn the shortest short straw and the strange girl with sharp teeth is exactly the impossible thing he knew she was the first moment he laid eyes on her. "Be still now," she tells him, and the kid smells roses and cinnamon, and he forgets all about the shotgun. "I want to show you something pretty," says Dancy. "I want to show you something precious. Why, I confess, first time I saw it, I bawled like a newborn baby with a bellyache, that's how goddamn pretty it is, what I'm about to let you see." And the hard man watches as she takes the boy, and all the others watch, and the night watches with all of its countless eyes, and the moon looks down and shudders, and the red dream rolls on.

6.

"It ain't like she's never afraid," says the one crow to the other crow, the two conversing crows perched in a dying, lightning-struck pecan tree. "It ain't like that at all. It's more like she ain't been nothin' but afraid for so long she now she lacks the requisite acumen and good sense god gave a crawdad to *know* that she's afraid." And the other crow, the one with a yellow stripe down its back, a coward crow, a highway crow, that crow narrows its beady amber eyes and nods its head and says, "Well, okay. I guess I see how that might be."

7.

Dreaming she's home, and home is the cabin on Eleanore Road, the cabin in Shrove Wood, dreaming maybe she's never left. But she isn't a child anymore. She isn't a child, and she might even be older than the girl that the seraph rode herd on for so long, driving her from bloody deed to bloody deed, from tragedy to tragedy. She sits on her bed, and she watches out the window, at afternoon fading very slowly towards twilight settling over the Florida panhandle wilderness. She can hear her mother busy in some other room, but the sound seems to come from far away. In this dream, the old cabin in Eleanore Wood has many rooms, not only the three, and also it isn't festooned with a hundred pairs of deer antlers and her grandmother and grandfather have both been dead a very, very long time, so it's only her mother and she who live there. Or at least she *thinks* these things are true. It seems that way, most of the time, though sometimes there are shadows who pass through the house like phantoms, and maybe they live there, as well, or maybe they're only the ghosts of people who lived in the cabin before she was born, before her mother was born, or they're people who *will* live here someday. Dancy watches the yard and the line where she and her mother hang the laundry – a sagging bit of baling wire strung between two metal rods – and she watches the line of palmetto and pines and underbrush that mark the end of the yard and the beginning of the woods.

"You ought'a shut that window," her mother calls out from somewhere deep in the vast labyrinthine cabin, but Dancy ignores her. It was such a hot day, a day just about hot enough to burn down the world, but now the air slipping in over the windowsill is cool and sweet and it smells like night-blooming flowers and pine straw. There's a whole constellation of fireflies out there, winking on and off, and the songs of cicadas and spring peepers and whippoorwills throb like a bad tooth.

And then there's a nervous, scrambling, scritching sort of a sound from right below the window, and it startles her before she has a chance to remind herself not to be afraid. It's only the ghoul, and the ghoul has never yet done her harm. Sometimes it comes to her at sunset, and sometimes they talk, and sometimes she just listens to the stories that it tells. The ghoul lives in a sinkhole beneath the cabin, a sinkhole that leads down to secret limestone caverns and wide ubterranean lakes where fat blind fish feed on blinder salamanders. The ghoul has never said whether there are other ghouls down there or if it's the only one, and Dancy has never thought to ask.

It scratches at the cabin walls, and she sits up a little straighter and leans a little nearer to the window. The ghoul never speaks much above a whisper.

"You there, girl?" it asks.

"You know I am," she replies. "Where else would I be?"

"Is that a riddle?" the ghoul wants to know, because the ghoul is extremely fond of riddles and sometimes it and Dancy make a game of them.

"No, it ain't a riddle. It was just a regular sort of question, is all." She pauses, then asks, "Did you bring me an offerin' tonight, ghoul? Did you bring me a gift? And you already know that also ain't no riddle."

"I do," says the ghoul, and then it reaches up with its long left arm, the wrinkled skin a patchwork of scabs and mold and filth, and it leaves something on the sill. Dancy has never seen much more of the ghoul than that one arm, that arm and that crooked-fingered left hand. So, she only has her imagination to fill in the rest.

"You mean that for me?" she asks.

"I do," says the ghoul. "I wouldn't mean it for anyone else I ever met."

On the windowsill is a stingy bouquet of tiny wildflowers – dandelions and shepherd's needle, ironweed and thistles – all tied up together with a dirty bit of twine.

"That's very sweet of you," says Dancy, and she takes the flowers from the windowsill. "No one else ever brung me flowers. Did you know that?"

"I did not," the ghoul replies. "A girl like you, why, I figure she must have more beaus than you can shake a stick at. I figure they must be lining up outside her door, just begging for a chance to leave behind some flowers."

Dancy watches the fireflies and she listens to the whippoorwill and sniffs at the ghoul's bouquet, breathing in the commingled flowe and maggoty smells, the one seeming almost exactly like the othe to her dreaming nose. Under her bed there's a cigar box half fillec with things the ghoul has brought and left on her windowsill: one rec wooden checker, a toy dog molded in hard black plastic, a bird skul and five silver dollars, a spent shotgun shell, a rosary with shiny onyx beads. And a few other less wholesome things, besides.

"Maybe when I'm awake," she says.

"Maybe what when you're awake?" asks the ghoul.

"Maybe when I'm awake, maybe then I got more beaus bringing me flowers than you could shake a stick at. You know, my momma says I shouldn't talk to you."

"I know," says the ghoul. "I hear her, whenever she tells you that."

"She don't mean nothin' by it," says Dancy.

"The hell she don't. If *you* had a pretty little slip of a daughter would *you* be wantin' her conversin' with the likes on me, some lep rous ne'er-do-well what just crawled up from under the floorboards stinkin' of rot and bourbon and I don't know what all else? You bes *believe* she meant somethin' by it."

"Well, be that as it may, she ain't always right," says Dancy, anc she sets the bouquet down on the quilt.

Outside, the ghoul makes an anxious, snuffling noise.

"What's more," it says, "if'n she ever goes and finds out how I'm the one what ate them last three cats and how I'm the one what's been stealin' her eggs and how I'm *also* the one tumped over the washtub that time before last, well…"

"She ain't never gonna find out any of them things," Dancy tell: the ghoul, trying to sound reassuring. "So, you stop worrying and tel me a story. I feel like hearing a story tonight, so you tell me one, o maybe I won't accept these flowers. Maybe I'll give 'em back and holc out for better."

"Better what?" the ghoul wants to know.

"Better flowers," she says. "One of them beaus of mine, I bet he'll come bearin' roses and petunias and daffodils, and then you'll *wish* you'd told me a story."

The ghoul snuffles again, and it sighs, and it scratches at the wall.

"What sort of story?" it asks.

"Any sort you got handy. I ain't feelin' especially particular tonight."

"Well, so long as I get to pick which one."

"I just said you do. But keep your voice down, ghoul. I don't want to have to tell my momma again that it was only me in here talkin' to myself. I don't like the worried look she gets whenever I have to tell her that."

"Well, all right," the ghoul says, speaking even more softly now, its voice like sandpaper and dead leaves. Dancy lays down on her bed beside the flowers as twilight fades and the room fills up with night, and the ghoul tells her a story about a werewolf and a blackbird and an albino girl waiting alone at a bus stop. Like most of the stories the ghoul tells her, this one has riddles.

8.

This is a dream of a dream of a memory of the summer day that Dancy Flammarion first laid eyes on the seraph, of the day she walked out the front door of the cabin in Shrove Wood, and the screen banged shut behind her, and she walked out onto the porch and down the four front steps to the dusty yard, and she looked through a hole punched in this world and straight into the roiling crucible at the heart of creation. The place where stars are first conceived long ages before they're born. The hammer fall of the gods who work the forge and the bellows, the gods and lesser things than gods, lesser than the

God she was taught to believe is the *only* god and for whom, after this day, would go to war. Down the steps flanked by the heavy yellow heads of sunflowers and by tomato plants, and Dancy looks up at the sky, because she heard something, a sound she will not ever even attempt to describe, a sound she would forget were she able, and out in the dusty yard one of the chickens squawks and bursts into flame. And then another. And then another. And then the tops of pines and the highest limbs of the big magnolia and the roof of the barn, and Dancy wants to turn and run back into the house but she doesn't, and she will not ever be able to say why she doesn't. She just doesn't. *One does not run from an angel,* she might say, were she ever pressed, only in this moment, in this dream of a dream of this moment, she does not yet know or only believe that she is seeing an angel. But she doesn't run. She stands there in the sandy, dusty yard outside the cabin staring at the sky ripped open and the white fire pouring out of the wound and taking shape.

This will blind me, she thinks. *Or I'll be dead. Didn't God tell Moses that can't no one ever look at the face of God and not die? Didn't he? Don't I know that?* And she reminds herself this is only an angel that she saw that day, not God, so she won't go blind and she won't die, but she'll want to do both. She'll look into the face of the seraph and wish that she never had been born, and when it speaks she'll sink to her knees in the dust and the sand and the weeds and pray for it to go fly away somewhere else and talk to some other lonesome girl with pink eyes and only a mother and grandmother and not ever anyone else for company.

"And you think all that really happened?" the boy wants to know, but this is later, weeks or months later, or all the way to the next summer, the night she was passing the Red Hot truck stop on her way to Savannah. There was this boy, and he asked her if she wanted a date, and she said no, she didn't want a damn date. What about just some fucking company he said, and it surprised her when she said yes,

Imost as much as she is surprised this day by looking up and seeing he sky on fire.

"I know it happened," she replies, she sitting close to him in the notel room, he on the floor, on dirty carpet the color of a dead blue ay. Dancy had never been inside a motel room before and hasn't been nside once since this night. It's the boy's room, and he took her back here, and he had a beer and she a Coca-Cola. He's told her how girls don't really do it for him anyway, and she has no idea what he meant.

"You don't think maybe it was just a bad dream? Or maybe you ust might have imagined it or something?"

"You don't believe in angels?"

"Not especially," he says.

"You don't believe in God?"

"Not especially, no."

There is only one lamp in the dingy room and too many shad-ows and wallpaper that matches the dead blue-jay carpet and there's a television and she tells the boy she's never seen a TV before, not up close. The air in the room smells like stale cigarette smoke and disinfectant and mold. There's air conditioning, but Dancy made him shut it off because, she said, a room ought not feel like February on a July night.

"You ain't even afraid of Hell?" she asks the boy.

"I can't be afraid of something I don't believe in."

If she lives to be a thousand years old, she will not forget the sight of the burning chickens dashing madly about the yard, streaming black smoke and burning feathers. She might remember the burning chickens even when she's forgotten the faces and wings and the terri-ble swift molten sword of the seraph.

"You don't believe the Bible?"

"We should talk about something else," he says.

And before this, back out in the Red Hot truck-stop parking lot, he asphalt cooling and all the huge diesel engines rumbling like the

sky cracking open and Dancy lugging her duffel bag, and the bo
steps out of the dark and asks if she wants a date.

Is this one of 'em? she asks the angel. *Did you bring me here to do fo
him like I done for all them others?*

"I shouldn't be lingerin' like this," Dancy tells the boy, whil
burning chickens dance about the dusty yard and the barn goes up i
flame. "I got places I'm supposed to be."

"Probably isn't any place that won't wait 'til morning," he says
and then, before she can argue, he starts in telling her about a plac
in Russia he read about in a book, a place called Tunguska, and ho
a hundred years ago something exploded in the sky above Tunguska
"Like a bomb," he said. "Like a nuclear bomb. And it knocked dow
more than eighty million trees, knocked 'em down flat like match
sticks. If it had happened over a big city, it would have been just lik
Hiroshima or Nagasaki."

Dancy has never heard of Hiroshima or Nagasaki, but she doesn'
ask him what they are. She just wants to be out of the room now. She jus
wants to be back on the road and not listening to this boy who doesn'
even believe he's going to Hell for not believing in the Word of God.

"I never heard of none of that," she tells him.

"It's the first thing came to mind when you told me about seein
the angel that first time, the white fire in the sky and the trees burnin
and all. That's the first thing I thought about, Tunguska."

"You read that in a book?" she asks.

"Yeah," the boy tells her, "a book about asteroids and falling star
and stuff. I'm thinking maybe that's what you saw that day, a meteo
burning up as it entered the atmosphere and fell to earth."

"The Russians don't believe in God, neither," she says, and th
boy frowns and now he turns his head and looks out the motel win
dow, instead of looking at Dancy. There's red light, bloody red ligh
from the Red Hot truck stop's towering neon sign, light to stain th
boy's face, so that's another thing that makes Dancy nervous.

When the chickens have finally stopped dancing about, there's nothing at all left of them but ash and hollow shards of charred chicken bone.

"I'm just about outta money," says the boy on the blue-jay carpet. "I had two hundred dollars when I started out, but now I'm just about flat fucking broke."

"Well, I ain't got no money, neither," Dancy tells him, which is almost the truth, except for one dollar and seventy-five cents hidden in her duffel bag.

"I set out for Nashville," he says. "Or maybe Memphis. But I've hardly gone a hundred miles, and here I am almost flat broke and turning tricks at a goddamn truck stop in Waycross, Georgia and I wasted money I do not have on a shitty motel room, because I'm afraid of sleeping in the woods."

"I shouldn't be here," Dancy says again, and she gets up to go. But that's when the boy shows her he has a gun, and that's when he says that if she's got any money at all she'd better hand it over. And that's when Dancy sees the seraph burning bright outside the motel window, burning like the pillar of fire leading the Israelites all the way to the Promised Land. And so that's when Dancy kills the boy, not because he was one of the monsters, but just because he's in the way.

The sky above Shrove Wood burns like the sky over Tunguska.

But Dancy Flammarion doesn't look away. It would be blasphemy to look away. It would be blasphemy to so much as shut her eyes.

The dead boy's gun isn't even loaded. She checks to be sure, after she's cut his throat, after the pillar of fire with all its blazing faces and with its six wings is gone again and she's alone and there's only the neon sign of the Red Hot truck stop. She checks, then leaves the gun on the bed. And this is her dream of a dream, nothing but a reflection of a reflection, only memories of memories. Dancy Flammarion falls to her knees in the dusty yard outside the cabin, and she leaves the boy where he fell. She walks back out into the muggy summer night, shutting the motel room's door behind her, and there are little smoldering piles of chicken cinders everywhere she steps.

9.

Behind her is all the fire that ever was, and before her is time and sleep and waking and the endless road. Even dreaming, these things are plain enough. Even dreaming, these things are brutally self-evident. There is also the pretty woman, still or again, and she walks beside Dancy Flammarion and she recites the lyrics of songs and also lines of poetry and quotations from the dead men and dead women. In the merciful, portable shadow beneath her umbrella, Dancy hides from the sun, and she walks and listens to the pretty woman with straw-colored hair and freckles and dirty fingernails and bare feet.

"All we see or seem," says the woman, "is but a dream within a dream."

"Who said that?" Dancy asks.

The pretty woman ignores the question and says, instead, "Those who dream by day are cognizant of many things which escape those who dream only by night."

Behind them, the angel howls, at least as terrible in dreams as to Dancy's waking eyes and ears and battered mind. Dancy walks down the broken white center line of the highway, because the asphalt at the edges of the road has gone soft in the heat and is beginning to bubble and steam. Once, her mother told her about tar pits and how long ages ago animals had become trapped in them and died, and it's all too easy for Dancy to imagine herself getting stuck and dragged down into the smothering, boiling darkness waiting beneath the road.

Overhead, the sky is filled with crows.

In dreams, I walk with you, the pretty woman sings. *In dreams, I talk with you.*

Dancy decides to ignore the pretty woman, because maybe if she ignores her long enough, the woman will get bored and go away to haunt somebody else's sleep.

The crows sound like thunder.

Dancy has decided it's best to ignore them, too. She thinks, *I should get off this road now. It's too hot and I'm too tired. I can rest. I can walk at night.* But on either side of the highway are towering, impenetrable green cathedrals of kudzu, honeysuckle, poison sumac and poison ivy and oak, cat briers, blackberry, drooping wisteria, and creeper vines. Even if she were lucky enough to make it across the river of bubbling pitch without going down to meet all those vanished mammoths and saber-toothed cats that didn't make it onto the Ark, there would still be that living green hell waiting to swallow her alive.

Sweet dreams of you, sings the pretty woman with straw-colored hair, *things I know can't come true. Why can't I forget the past...*

Sweat stings Dancy's eyes, and she wipes her face with the back of the hand that isn't holding the black umbrella, and she says, "One day, angel, you're gonna have worn me down to just bare bone and gristle, and then there won't be nobody left to do your biddin' no more. If you don't ease up, that day's gonna be sooner rather than later. What you gonna do then? Toss me aside and find another?"

The crows bleed lightning.

And possibly then for the very first time ever, waking or dreaming or any place in between, the seraph relents and deigns to answer one of Dancy Flammarion's questions, questions that have always been few and far between. Because it comes to her suddenly and in a flash that maybe *that's* who the pretty woman is, that maybe she's the ghost of some *other* lost girl, drowned in tar, cut down in battle, left for the crows and the worms and forgotten even by the Kingdom of Heaven. Someone else who once was the red right hand of the angel. Someone else who went where she was told, who did the killing and cleansed the land with fire and steel and blind righteous faith. Who *believed* because the only alternative to believing was too awful to contemplate

A dream is a wish your heart makes, the pretty woman sings, and her voice splashes the bright day like raindrops, and the soles of her feet sizzle against the scalding road like salt pork in an iron skillet.

Might be, she's near as I'll ever have to a sister. Might be she's something worse.

"Fine," says Dancy, and she takes a quartzite pebble from her jeans pocket and puts it in her mouth to tease a little saliva from her cheeks, some meager balm against the endless thirst. "If you really got nowhere better to be than here, I reckon you can tag along with me. I mean, I ain't gonna try to make you go. But you gotta keep up, and also you gotta not get in the way. You think you can manage that?"

And when the pretty woman doesn't answer her, Dancy realizes she's alone again, alone in this dream of the road from *here* to *there,* alone except for the seraph and the blistering, blinding summer day, alone except for the bubbling pitch and the towering green and all the hungry black thunderstorm birds wheeling restless overhead.

DREAMS OF A POOR WAYFARING STRANGER

Seven dreams, framed by an eighth. Mostly, this is me having fun with unrealized realities, though I think there's a lot of true shit about Dancy in these dream sequences. But dreams are often the couriers of our most inconvenient truths, aren't they? I could have titled this one "The Dream-Quest of Dancy Flammarion," but saner heads prevailed.

Requiem
(October 2018)

For half a night and most all of an autumn day, the blue-and-silver bus has ferried the slight, green-eyed woman along grey Southern highways beneath low-slung grey Southern skies. The bus left Savannah a little after midnight, departing the Greyhound station on Oglethorpe Avenue and rumbling north and west along the asphalt ribbon of I-16, racing the twin glare of its own headlights past Macon and a dozen other sleeping towns and all the way to Atlanta, farther north than the woman had ever been before. A six-wheeled carriage of diesel-scented steel passing through darkness to muddy daybreak to a rainy morning and then a stormy afternoon, before finally turning west and south towards Birmingham. Whenever the bus stopped – disgorging a few passengers, swallowing up a few others – the slight, green-eyed woman kept her seat, too afraid that if she were to dare get off, even just to stretch her legs for five minutes or have a cigarette or buy a bottle of Dr. Pepper, she'd never find the courage to get back on again.

And then where would I be? Why, then I'd be nowhere at all.

It took the better part of five years to find the courage to buy a ticket and pack a suitcase and board the night bus. When she was very young, she had imagined that she was brave and bold and audacious. When she had lived in the rotten, rambling mansion on East Hall Street with Miss Aramat Drawdes and the other ladies who'd styled themselves the Stephens Ward Tea League and Society of Resurrectionists, when she was hardly yet even nineteen years old, way back then she'd imagined herself just about the bravest, boldest, most audacious girl in the whole wide world. But way back then, way back twenty long years ago, what she'd known about the whole wide world would have fit in a brass thimble, with plenty of room left over for her or anyone else's thumb. Back then, she'd called herself Isolde Penderghast, a name she'd found written on the back of an old photograph, and she had played at being a monster. They'd all of them played at monstrosity, the nine women who'd lived together in the ancient house, and they'd even been permitted to rub shoulders with monstrous things and do the bidding of monstrous things, only to learn too late that they themselves were nothing more than sadly preposterous imitations and that all the *real* monsters laughed at them whenever their backs were turned.

A dazzling bright flash of lightning, lightning like the cloudy sky split apart by white atomic fire, and the slight, green-eyed woman flinches and shuts her eyes.

The young man in the seat beside her wants to know if she's okay.

"I don't like lightning, that's all," she says.

"My sister was like that. She hated thunderstorms. When we were kids, she'd hide beneath her bed. My sister, she thought thunderstorms meant the angels in Heaven were angry. The lightning terrified her."

And now the woman opens her eyes again, blinking back dancing afterimages left there by the lightning. For a moment or two, she stares silently at the young man, her heart racing and her mouth gone dust dry, trying to decide if that's really all he is, a young man on a bus, or if he might be something worse. He might well be, for all she knows, something much, *much* worse in disguise and his choice of words – *the angels in Heaven were angry* – was a slip of the mask, intentional or accidental. He might only be a young man whose sister is frightened of thunderstorms, or he might be something that's crawled aboard the bus to taunt her.

Maybe even something sent to see that she never reaches Birmingham.

The young man tells her his name, and she tells him that she's tired and isn't really in the mood for conversation. He apologizes and goes back to reading the paperback he was reading before the lightning startled her.

"But I'm not afraid of it," she says.

"You mean the lightning?" the young man asks. "But you just said –"

"What I said is that I don't like it. I didn't say it scares me."

He nods and says, "Okay, I see," without even bothering to look up from his book. She thinks about maybe moving to a different seat, but that would only draw attention, which might be exactly the wrong thing to do. So she just sits there instead, watching the stormy Alabama day, all the unfamiliar trees and the cars and trucks and the low Appalachian foothills, the raindrops spattering the Greyhound's window and then winding like tiny rivers across the glass. After only a few minutes, she nods off and dreams that the bus is a steamship crossing an ocean or a very great lake, and the waves that rise and fall and crash against the hull are all the vivid shades of October leaves. Whenever she looks over her shoulder towards the stern, she can see the multitude of ghosts trailing out behind the ship, swept along in its wake, caught and helpless to escape, dim, half-translucent phantoms that make her think of darting birds with the faces of women. She doesn't ever let herself look at them very closely or for very long. There are too many faces there she would recognize.

The young man with the paperback book is standing beside her on the wooden deck of the steamship. He asks, "Are they all yours?"

"Not all of them," she lies. "Not every single one."

"If it had been me," he says, "I'd have found a way to leave them behind. There must have been plenty of places you could have buried them. There must have been opportunities."

"It seemed like we were always *unburying* them," she tells him, then immediately wishes that she hadn't.

"Well," he says, "I don't know anything about that. I don't know, and I don't want to know. I got plenty enough problems without someone else's ghosts."

"They're not *all* mine," she says again, so quietly that she's almost whispering. "Well, I mean they're not all *only* mine."

"I don't think that makes much of a difference," he says, then walks away and leaves her standing there alone. She glances down at the water and finds that it's no longer stained the oranges and yellow gold and deep, deep reds of fallen autumn leaves, and there are no longer any waves, either. There isn't even a ripple now. The ocean or the lake has gone smooth and still as silvered glass, and her reflection stares back up at her with nervous sage-green eyes set into a face that looks a little older than it is, well into her forties, instead of hardly even thirty-nine, a face framed in tangled mouse-brown hair beginning to go grey at the temples. She lifts a thin hand to her throat and runs her fingers across all the little scars there. Behind the steamship, the ghosts wail and call out her *true* name, and they promise that all she has to do is climb over the railing and let herself fall and drown and then she'll never be lonely again.

It would be the easiest thing in the world.

It would be a blessing.

"I don't think I believe you," she says. "I think you're trying to deceive me."

We would not ever lie to you, wail the ghosts. *We would never lie to someone who once loved us so and who still hauls us around like cankers in her heart.*

"Go away," she says, and her reflection in the water says exactly the same thing.

And then where would we be? the ghosts all moan and wail in unison. *Why, then we'd be nowhere at all.*

"Well, that's too bad, because I don't want you anymore."

You know she'll kill you, that one, wail the ghosts. *You know she'll kill you dead.*

"Go *away*, I said," and no sooner have the words left her lips and also the lips of her reflection than there's a terrific thunderclap and *then* lightning, thunder and lightning coming at her the wrong way round, and the slight woman with sage-green eyes whose right name never has been Isolde Penderghast comes awake to the squeal and whine of the Greyhound's air brakes as the bus shudders to a stop somewhere in downtown Birmingham. It's almost dark now and still raining, or it's raining again, and she waits until everyone else has gone before she finds the courage she needs to get up from her seat and walk down the narrow aisle and exit the bus.

(June 2013)

"I'm very tired, that's all. I hate airplanes, and I've been stuck on them all day, and I'm very tired," and then Biancabella sits down at the dingy table in the dingy little kitchenette while Isolde Penderghast – she of the stolen name, she who dreams of steamships and ghosts – stands at the rust-stained sink and runs tap water into a dented cherry-red kettle. "It wasn't necessary for you to come, not all the way down here from Rhode Island," she says to Biancabella. "You could have sent a letter, or you could have called me. A phone call would have been fine, or a letter. I honestly didn't mean for you to come all this way. And I know how you hate airplanes. I remember that." Biancabella looks so much older than she'd expected, the wrinkles and her close-cropped hair like snow, but then, she's a good fifteen years older than the green-eyed woman. Biancabella opens her purse and takes out a half-empty pack of Marlboros. She lights a cigarette, blows smoke towards the ceiling, then looks about for an ashtray. "Kid," she says, "you don't answer questions like that in letters. You definitely don't answer questions like that over the phone. I know it's been a while, but I thought we taught you better than that." Isolde shrugs, then squeezes herself between the refrigerator and the table and Biancabella to open the narrow window at one end of the room. Wood squeals against wood and a few flakes of white-grey paint come loose and pepper the linoleum floor at her feet. The night air smells like car exhaust and hot streets and much more faintly of honeysuckle blossoms. Isolde takes a saucer from the cabinet, chipped Wedgwood blue, and sets it down on the table in front of Biancabella. She takes out two more saucers and two cups, then goes back to the stove to wait for the kettle to boil. "Are you even sure this is what you want?" Biancabella asks her, and yeah, that's her real name because her mother was a literature professor at Tulane and she had a thing for Italian fairy tales. "If it weren't, you'd have come all this way for nothing," says Isolde. Biancabella frowns and takes another drag on her cigarette. This time she blows the smoke out the open window. "That wasn't exactly an answer," says Biancabella, tapping ash into the Wedgwood saucer, and Isolde sighs and says, "Yes, Bee, I'm sure it's what I want. I wouldn't have asked you if I weren't sure." The kettle starts to whistle, and she shuts off the burner. She puts a tea bag in each mismatched cup, Earl Grey for herself and black Darjeeling for Biancabella, then pours in the steaming water. "It has been my experience that people don't always know what they really want," Biancabella tells her. "And they pretty much never fucking know what's in their best interest. By the way, I have to ask, was it you who torched the house?" Isolde doesn't answer the question right away. She stands at the counter, still staring into the two cups. "Frankly, I don't care one way or the other," says Biancabella, and then she touches the ugly, crooked scar that runs from the corner of her mouth up her left cheek and almost to her ear. "You could burn down this whole fucking city, do what William Tecumseh Sherman *should* have done in 1864, and it'd be just fine by me. But Candida, she dreamt it was you, and she won't shut up about it. Which is why I'm asking." Isolde stands there staring into the cups and chewing her lower lip, worrying now at her own scars, at the delicate, crisscrossing roadmap traced upon her throat with a straight razor by a woman who's been dead almost fifteen years, straight-razor cuts to pass for kisses from the madwoman who took Isolde in off the streets, killed by an antique revolver that blew up in her hands, burying a white-hot chunk of shrapnel in her brain and splitting open Biancabella's cheek in the bargain. "Lots of people burn down houses," Isolde says. "I'm many things, but I'm not an arsonist." And Biancabella tells her not everyone who sets fire a house is an arsonist, how there's no end of houses in the world in need of burning, in need of being put out of their misery and everyone else's. "Sick houses," she says, and Isolde says, "Well, anyway, it wasn't me who did it," and she tries to pretend that's the truth. She carries the two cups and two tarnished teaspoons balanced on the two saucers over to the table, sets them both down, then sits across from Biancabella. Her chair squeaks, and it tilts a bit to one side because there's one front leg that's too short. But the chairs and the table came with the apartment, and it's not like she can afford to go out and buy furniture of her own. Biancabella reaches back into her purse and takes out a lavender envelope, and she slides it across the table. "Don't open it now," she says. "Don't open it until I'm all the way back in Providence." Isolde asks why and what difference it makes when she opens the envelope, whether Biancabella is there or not, and Biancabella tells her because those are the rules, that's why. She says, "When it's you sticking your neck out, you can set the terms." Isolde starts to reach for the envelope, but then decides there isn't any point, not as long as Biancabella is here in Savannah, not if she isn't yet allowed to open it and read what's inside. Biancabella takes another drag on her Marlboro, blows more smoke towards the open window, and then she removes the tea bag from her cup. "You *know* she'll kill you, right?" she asks Isolde. "That one, she might not be who or what she was when the Bailiff came round that night, but that doesn't mean she won't still do it if you give her the chance." Isolde takes two sugar cubes from the bowl on the table and drops them into her own cup, not bothering to take out the tea bag first. "I know," she says. "But maybe people aren't so very different from houses, not when you get right down to it, and maybe some of them just need to be put out of their misery. Maybe that's all I am, Bee, a sick house waiting for somebody to do me the kindness of burning me down." Biancabella scowls at her and takes a tentative sip of the black Darjeeling, but it's still too hot to drink and she scalds her tongue. "Shit," she hisses, setting the cup back down so quickly that a little tea sloshes out onto the dingy tabletop. She turns her head away and glares at the window, instead of glaring at Isolde. "Don't you do that," she says. "Don't do what?" Isolde asks, and Biancabella says, "Don't you twist my own words around on me like that," she replies. "And if all you're after is suicide, you don't have to be half so goddamn dramatic about it. There are easier ways." Isolde stops stirring her tea, already wishing she could take back what she said, not even sure she meant it. "Anyway," she says, "it's so good to see you again. I wish that you could stay more than just the one night. I haven't seen any of us in so awfully long. I was beginning to think possibly I never would and all I'd ever have left are memories." Biancabella's hand goes to her scarred cheek again, and she says, "I shouldn't have come here at all. I wasn't going to. I meant never to come within five hundred miles of this accursed place ever again. But when I burned your letter –" Then before she can finish the thought, Isolde interrupts her. "I'm sorry," she says. "I really, really *am* sorry. But I didn't know who else to ask. I didn't know how to reach anyone but you." Biancabella laughs a dry, not-quite humorless laugh and mutters something about her fucking luck, and when she sees how she's smoked the Marlboro almost down to the filter, she lights another one off the butt.

(October 2018)

In her big house at the foot of Red Mountain, in the room she spent a week painting black, the room with blacked-out windows and chalk drawings scrawled crude as Cro-Magnon cave paintings on the walls and ceiling, Dancy Flammarion sleeps, and sleeping she dreams of another life, the life that condemned her to *this* life, carelessly banging it together from weathered grey pine slats and tar paper and rusted nails. The life that again and again and *again* promised her the unending peace of paradise when the best it ever really had to deliver on all those promises was one or another sort of hell. And sleeping and dreaming that *other* life, that vanished *before*, that prologue which now seems brief and thin as dawn, she dreams of crumbling brick chimneys rising from antebellum ruins, of the stench of river mud and catfish and salamanders, and of the girl who did not live long enough to become a woman and who was, by the time Dancy found her, no longer even a girl anymore. No longer even human or breathing or a heart beating in her chest, but only a starving husk of a girl left behind by history and fate to sleep away the summer days and the winter days beneath restless dark water and at night to wander the fallow, forsaken land that once had been the cotton fields and peach orchards of her father's plantation.

The night throbs with the songs of cicadas and frogs and the shrill calls of night birds, and the girl asks, *Have you come all this long way just for me?* and Dancy catches something unmistakably *hopeful* in the question, in that lonesome dead voice, something *wishful*. The girl is naked, save the slime and filth of the river bed, and the mist above the fields kindly twists about the vampire like a gauzy winding shroud. *You cannot imagine, Miss Dancy, how long it's been since anyone has come to call on me.*

You wouldn't believe me if I told you.

Behind Dancy, the seraph is a whirling pillar of fire, tall as the sky, and the knife in her hand feels almost heavy as a sledgehammer.

"I see to this one, this *last* one," Dancy says, "then from here on, I'll do my own dirty work, angel, and you'll do yours."

If the girl from the river heard even a single word that Dancy said, she makes no sign that she's heard. Instead, she looks up at the great vault of the summer sky, her hungry silver eyes drinking in the moonlight and starlight and even the faint specks of planets, of Mars and Jupiter and Venus, and it seems to Dancy that she must be just about the most lost thing that ever was.

The Captain says there are Yankees in Chattanooga. He says they'll be in Atlanta by July or sooner. Can you even comprehend such a thing? You'll stay for supper, of course. We haven't much these days, I'm afraid, but what we have we'll share.

There's a dead rat clutched in the girl's right hand, hanging there limp and broken and sucked all but dry. She stops gazing at the sky and holds the dead rat out to Dancy. The girl smiles, and her teeth are charcoal pegs set into charcoal gums.

"The *last* one," Dancy says again, weary words spoken through gritted teeth, and the seraph roars, and the earth shudders and all the night shudders, too. Then the knife does what the knife does, and the dead girl from the river comes apart like a doll made of dust and cinders, and all that remains of her is carried away on the wind.

The seraph roars.

And twenty years farther on, in *this* life, this tawdry aftermath of *that* life, Dancy Flammarion opens her eyes. Just like always, there's the sudden, ugly shock of waking, of falling out of the dream and slamming pell-mell, ass over tits back into *here* and *now*. Before she fell asleep, she'd switched on the thrift-store lamp on the floor beside the mattress, so at least there's the glow of that 40-watt bulb to halfway hold the black walls at bay. She shields her eyes and squints up at all the terrible things she's drawn on those walls, all the things she hunted down and put an end to because the angel said that's the reason she'd been born, the *only* reason she'd been born. To slay the wicked. To balance the scales. Dancy lies breathless and sweating on the bare mattress, her back and neck stiff and aching, staring up at all her murders and straining to hear whatever it was that woke her.

You wouldn't believe me if I told you.

And there it is – a knock at the door.

And then the doorbell that she didn't even know still worked.

If I lay here very still, they'll go away, she thinks. *Whoever it is, eventually they'll get tired of knockin' and mashin' that bell and go away, and then I can go back to sleep. It ain't no one I know, 'cause I don't know anyone, and if it is someone I know, they can come back some other time.*

Leave me alone. Go away.

I don't even hear you.

You cannot imagine, Miss Dancy, how long it's been since anyone has come to call on me.

Whoever it is knocks again, harder than before, more insistently than before.

"Go away," Dancy says very quietly. "Just please go away." On one of the black walls, near the door leading out to the hallway, the trio of bat-winged werewolves she's drawn there snarl and leer and seem to laugh at her. She only almost says, *I wasn't talkin' to you three, so just shut the hell up.*

But only almost.

She thinks about closing her eyes again and pretending she's still asleep.

"No one says I *gotta* go down and see who it is," she whispers to herself and not the werewolves and not any of the other monsters drawn on the walls. "No one says I gotta go answer that damn door, not if I don't *want* to. Not if I don't *mean* to. Ain't no one out there I *need* to see, and ain't no one there I *want* to talk to. There sure ain't no one out there who needs to talk to *me*."

Have you come all this long way just for me?

"Go away," Dancy says again, and again the doorbell rings.

Little pig, little pig, let me come in, one of the werewolves snickers, and she imagines the other two think that's so funny that they're rolling around on the wall now, laughing so hard they're holding onto their bellies so they won't bust a gut.

Whoever it is knocks again.

And again.

And finally Dancy Flammarion gives up and goes to answer the door…

…and here I am on *her* doorstep, the doorstep I have been assured is *her* doorstep, the doorstep of this tall Mardi-Gras colored house – purple for justice, green for faith, a shade of yellow that may as well be gold to stand for power – and I have walked the wet streets of this city all night long, hours and hours until *this* morning hour. I have left the sidewalk and crossed the tiny yard and stepped between the two crape myrtle trees. I have rung this doorbell and rapped on this door until my knuckles are beginning to ache because my only other option is turning right round again and finding my way back to the bus stop downtown, and *how* is that an option when I no longer even have a place to live in Savannah, because this was always meant to be a one-way trip. I knock on the door again, and again no one answers. I stare up at the oddly grotesque house painted purple, green, and gold, gaudy as I would expect from any good Victorian housepainter still reeling from the revelation of aniline dyes. A house with as many windows as this house has, with as many eyes, it ought to feel as though it's staring back at me, wondering who is this stranger banging on its door. But heavy draperies have been drawn across every single pane of glass that I can see, and maybe that's only to keep out the sweltering Alabama sun, but maybe there's some other reason entirely. So, a *blind* house painted the colors of Mardi Gras, a *blinded* house, weighted down by so many pediments and dormers and Italiante flourishes, waiting for a parade that isn't ever coming. I look at the house, and it *doesn't* stare back into me, because it can't *see,* and I'm wondering all over again, as I have found myself wondering so many times since Biancabella left and I opened her envelope, the envelope she'd brought all the way from New England, and I read that address – first quietly to myself and then aloud – wondering if there's any particular reason I should believe this is the *right* house. It might not be. It doesn't *have* to be. Whoever she paid to find the answer to my question, maybe they got it wrong, or maybe they lied to her, maybe they took her money but the whole thing was a con. Or maybe, instead, Biancabella picked some house at random from some random list of addresses, because she doesn't *want* me to do this thing, and it's not as though I could blame her. I knock on the door again, and this time, *this time* I hear a noise from the other side, the faint but unmistakable sound of movement from within the Mardi-Gras house, and I think, *This is my last chance to not do it. This is my last chance to change my mind and run away and leave well enough alone and let sleeping dogs sleep once and for all like Merlin in his crystal caves.* I think, *What Biancabella said, maybe she's exactly right, she'll kill you, that one, she'll do for you just like she did for Aramat, only that isn't the way it happened,* I protest, *not really. It was Aramat who pulled the trigger of that old gun. It was Aramat who was her own undoing.* And I imagine Biancabella asking right back, *You really believe that, kid? After all you saw back in the day, you really believe there wasn't some other force at work that morning than mere mundane physics, ordinary mechanical mishaps, whatever happens when you try to fire a revolver that hasn't been fired or even fucking cleaned in half a century, something more terrifying and divine than maybe grime or a bullet lodged in the barrel?* But at least I don't have to think of an answer, or repeat some answer back to myself that I invented on the long bus ride from the Georgia low country or all that time I spent walking and waiting for sunup and a decent hour to come knocking on *her* door. Because now there's the rattle of a chain latch being slid from its track, the dull thud of a deadbolt lock being turned, and then the purple, green, and gold door opens – not only a cautious inch or two, but it opens all the way, opening on cool hallway shadows and dusty floorboards. And here she is, after all this time, after twenty long years come and gone, here she is, barefoot and wrapped in a mustard-yellow terry-cloth bathrobe, and I can tell she's squinting at the daylight despite the sunglasses. Her skin is even paler than I remember, her fine white hair grown long and plaited into a braid that hangs halfway down her back. And the first thing I feel at the sight of her is surprise, though not surprise that I've actually found the albino girl the Bailiff brought to the house that night in 1998, the girl who talked to angels and slew lions and tigers and bears, oh my. No, surprise that she's *aged,* that she has not somehow remained just exactly the same as she was that night and that morning all those years ago, a fly caught in amber, immortality her reward for bloody services rendered. And these are the things I'm thinking about when she says to me, "I don't talk to Mormons. I don't talk to Jehovah's Witnesses, either. And I don't buy things from people who knock at my door, and I also don't vote." Her voice makes me think of vellum rubbed between thumb and forefinger until it's almost rubbed straight through. And I say to her, "You don't remember me, do you?" But then she wouldn't, and if the truth be told, I never actually expected that she would. "No," she says. "I *don't* know you. I've never seen you before in my life, and I ain't got anything to say to you, neither. So go away or I'll go back inside and all the police." Then *I* say to *her,* "The big house in Savannah, the place where you were brought late one night and where you opened an old bottle filled with light, and what you let out of that bottle, it saved you from a thing that was only playing at being a pretty boy in a dress, a thing that was afraid of opening the bottle for itself." I say *all* that, and I say it a little bit too fast, because I've rehearsed the words so many times now, choosing them carefully and reciting them over and over and over to myself. And she watches me from her doorway, and she takes a deep breath and pulls the robe a little more tightly about herself, against memories maybe or only against the October morning chill, and after she's quiet for another few moments she says, "There was a talkin' black bear A talkin' bear wearin' a red fez," and I nod my head. I probably nod too eagerly, and never mind that not once did I hear that moldering taxidermy utter even a lone syllable. "Yes," I say. "There was a bear. My name was Isolde back then. I mean, I *called* myself Isolde. I was the youngest that night." She takes a step back from the door. "You were all goin' to eat me," she says, and for some reason, the *way* she says it, I want to laugh. I want very badly to laugh, but I know better. "Yeah," I say. "That was us. Cannibals in lacy frocks." And I also take a step back, retreating a step, giving her room, marveling that I'm not afraid. "What do you want?" she asks. "Why'd you come here? Who I was back then, I ain't that person anymore. I think you should go now." And I tell her, "I only want to talk. I swear to you, that's all. I just want to talk." She pushes the sunglasses a little farther up the bridge of her nose. "Well, it just so happens I ain't got nothin' to say," she says, "not to you or to any of the rest of them. I done already told you already, that's not who I am no more." And I say to her, "I'm not who I was, either. But I still want to talk to you, and that's all, like I said, just talk, because on that night we *were* who we were —" and before I can say more, Dancy Flammarion abruptly relents and steps aside and motions for me to enter the Mardi-Gras colored house, and so that's what I do, before she changes her mind.

(July 1998)

It was still daylight when she sat down on this log at the muddy edge of the muddy Altamaha River, still almost an hour to go before dusk, but now the sun's down and the waxing moon is rising above the slash pines and black-gum branches and bald cypresses shaggy with Spanish moss. At her back are the kudzu- and wisteria-strangled ruins of a planation burned to the ground during Sherman's long march to the sea, torched when Dancy's great-great-great-grandfathers were still young men going to war or dead on blood-soaked battlefields or hiding out in the vast Okefenokee wilderness to avoid Confederate conscription. Like most nights along the river, most nights in these fields and forests, this night is alive with ghosts and bad memories, and all those many decades ago might almost have been only yesterday. Dancy finishes carving her name into the log, then slips the rusted butcher knife back into the top of her left boot and rolls down the cuff of her jeans to hide the handle.

"I knew right off how it was you," says the huge alligator floating only seven or eight feet from shore. "Right off, I knew it surely couldn't be nobody else *but* you."

"I shouldn't be talkin' to gators," Dancy says, and she runs her fingers along the marks she's made in the rotting log. "I think that's statin' the obvious."

The alligator makes an annoyed rumbling sound way down in its throat or its belly and drifts a little closer. It blinks its eyes and says "Well, maybe that's so, but it works both ways, now don't it just. And maybe was I you, lurkin' round and fit to pass for some kinda haint myself, I *might* not be so quick to be particular who I found myself conversatin' with. Word is, you ain't got too many friends, white girl."

The possum sitting at the far end of the log from Dancy stops gnawing at a half-eaten bullfrog and licks its lips and smacks its muzzle and says to the alligator, "Now, now, don't get riled. Probably, she idn't mean nothin' by it. Most folks ain't accustomed to talkin' with ou cold-blooded sons-a-bitches, that's all. It don't come easy-like to m." And then to Dancy, the possum says, "Is it true you done come or the gal in the water? Is that a natural born fact?"

"I'm sure that's not any of *your* business," Dancy replies, and now he's squinting into the darkness, trying to keep up with the alligaor, because for all she knows it hasn't eaten tonight. Or hasn't eaten nough. For all she knows, it's only bothering to talk to her so it can hrow her off guard and get in close enough to drag her into the river.

"We *live* here," says the alligator. "*You,* you're just passin' through. Ve're the ones what gotta fret every night if maybe *this* is the night he'll be comin' for *our* gizzards, so maybe, on further reflection, you an see how you might be confused on that count."

"I never met an alligator that talked so much," says Dancy.

"But *is* it true you come for her?" the possum asks again, pressng the question instead of going back to eating the bullfrog. "Is it rue you done heard tell of her deeds and depredations agin us simple olk, and here you are to right the wrongs, like you done did up in Vaycross and Bainbridge and I don't even know where all else?"

"I go where the angel tells me to go," Dancy says. "It ain't my say. \nd you, Mr. Gator, you best mind your distance or maybe it'll turn ut you're the one I've come for."

The alligator snorts and narrows its eyes and it tells her how it's lready had two fine, fat turtles and a right tasty bullhead catfish onight and she shouldn't flatter herself.

"I mean it," Dancy says, starting to think maybe she shouldn't ave been so quick to put the knife away, and she's about to reach or it again, when the possum scrambles down off the log, getting in etween her and the alligator.

"Quit it," the possum hisses, "right now this very minute, the oth of you," and then it looks up at Dancy, cross-eyed and with a tringy bit of frog guts stuck in its whiskers. "So if it's that angel of

yours calls the shots, I reckon what I mean to be askin' is did it send
you here tonight because of the gal in the water."

"Maybe," says Dancy.

"Well, I *hope* it's more'n maybe," the possum says, "but also that
would be a pleasant startlement, is all, 'cause way I heard it told by an
otter lives down the slough from here, it's only human-type folks you
and that angel look out for, not us poor, dumb lowborn critters, which
is all that gal in the water ever bothers with."

Dancy chews at her right thumbnail a moment, then looks from
the possum, past the spot where she's pretty certain the alligator i
floating, at the wide bend in the Altamaha, the water sliding by slow
and smooth and dark as blackstrap molasses. The place where sh
was told the dead girl sleeps when the sun's in the sky, wrapped up ir
the cold mud at the very bottom of the river, dreaming her hungry
red dreams.

"You're sayin' she don't eat folks?" asks Dancy.

"Not *human*-type folks," the possum replies. "Not that I eve
heard tell. I mean, there ain't *that* many of your sort around here t
keep the likes of her fed and happy."

And then the alligator chuckles its throaty wet alligator chuckle
and it says, "See, now, Mr. Possum, I done did already *told* you that'
how it was, and here it is you're hearin' the very same damn thing
from her very own damn lips. Folks like us, we see after our own
selves, or our own selves they don't get seen after. Why, white girl,
bet you've dined on at least your own fair share of gator *and* possum
or else muck ain't mucky an' shit don't stink."

"No, no, no, *no,*" the possum says, and now it's sitting up on
its hind legs, wringing its forepaws, looking about as worried as
possum can look. "You please say that ain't the truth, Miss Danc
Flammarion. You say how it *matters* to you and how it matters to tha
angel, too, if simple folks suffer, that it ain't only God's own choser
what get the benefit of heavenly swift swords when things like that ga

n the water, *wrong* things what ain't got no business even bein', are nvolved. Please, you say that's true."

"She ain't gonna say it," mutters the alligator, "'cause it *ain't* true."

"But don't the Good Book say how don't a single sparrow fall to the ground without Heaven knowin' all about it?"

"Says they *know,*" the alligator grunts. "Don't never say how they cares."

"I am worth *many* sparrows," Dancy says, and she gets up from her log and hefts the heavy duffel bag back onto her shoulder and finds where she left her umbrella leaning against a cypress stump.

"Where you goin' now?" the possum wants to know.

"That's somethin' else I figure ain't exactly none of your business," Dancy says. "Now good night to the both of you, good night and good luck," and then she's gone so fast it's almost as if she were never there, except for her name carved on the log and her boot prints in the mud.

"What I done told you," says the alligator.

"It ain't fair," says the possum, "us not matterin' like that."

"Ah, calm yourself," the alligator grumbles. "Like they says, don't take life so serious. It ain't nohow permanent." And then the reptile sinks back into the depths of blackwater, leaving only a momentary swirl and tiny ripples to lap at the clumps of cattail and pickerelweed growing along the shore. The possum sits staring forlornly at the place on the log where Dancy isn't sitting anymore, and then it sighs a weary, defeated possum sigh and goes back to what's left of the bullfrog.

(October 2018)

I'm closing the front door, shutting away the scalding path of light, the path by which I have permitted her to enter, and the door latches with a click like the hammer of a revolver clicking into place before the trigger's squeezed. Before the boom. Before thunder and lightning, and I'm thinking over and over, *Why have I let her in? I didn't have to do that. I didn't have to stand aside when I had already told her to go away and leave me be.* I'm thinking these things as I lead her past the steps leading upstairs and down the hallway towards the kitchen, because the kitchen seems the most safe of all my few possibilities. *Why have I let her in? I didn't have to do that. Why have I let her in? I didn't have to do that.* Over and over, like that, and I see the way *she* sees the walls. I see the way she looks at all the things I have painted there down all the years I have lived in this house at the bottom of the mountain, all my stories, all the words copied from my Bible or from my books or from the inside of my head. She doesn't stop to read or stare, because I think she believes that she is too mannerly for that and is afraid she will offend me and maybe tip her hand. Or she's just trying to be polite. I don't know. I *can't* know. Which is why I shouldn't have let her inside my house. Which is why I should have slammed the door and if she didn't go away called the police to come and carry her off. There's a witch at my front door. There's a cannibal. There's a woman who keeps the counsel of monsters, and who lays with other women, and a long, long time ago she tried to eat me. Yes, that's what I said, and yes, she did. But I let her in my house, and she's walking down the hallway of my house looking at the thoughts on my walls, *Why have I let her in? I didn't have to do that. Why have I let her in? I didn't have to do that.* And though she does not stop and gawk or read the words long written there, when she passes the door that goes down to the cellar she does ask me, "Did you paint all of these?" I don't know how she meant the words, but they ring in my ears like an accusation, and her voice rings like a church bell in my head, and I almost find the courage to say let's walk backwards to the front door and you go back outside and I'll lock it behind you and never open it again for anyone, much less ghosts of nights so evil I almost did not live to see the day again. "They're remarkable," she says, and I keep my eyes on the floor, the wood grain nd scuff marks, the dust and paint spatters, and she says, "I never new you were an artist." I tell her that I'm not an artist, and she looks back over her shoulder at me, though I can't see her do it, because I'm busy staring at the floor. But I can feel her grey-green eyes like lichen clinging to rock, and so she wants to know who painted the pictures, f I wasn't the one, and have I ever heard of someone named Howard Finster. "I painted them," I say, "but that don't make me no artist." We're still walking, but those eyes, those eyes on me, and how can someone walk without looking where they're going, and why didn't I stay in the black room with the werewolves, and why did I let her into my house? "Not just anyone could have done this," she says, and here's me, wanting her to stop talking, but she won't, and I'm trying to remember how many steps it is from the front door to the kitchen and shouldn't we be there by now? "It takes someone who can see," she says, and almost I say, *And another angel came out of the temple, crying with a loud voice to him that sat on the cloud, Thrust in thy sickle, and reap: for the time is come for thee to reap; for the harvest of the earth is ripe.* Only I don't, because the words would fall not on deaf ears, but on ears that will *not* hear. I almost say, *The seven stars are the angels of the seven churches: and the seven candlesticks which thou saw are the seven churches,* only that would have not been any better. And now we've gone far enough that I can see the place where the hallway leads you either to the kitchen at my right hand or straight on to the back porch and all my Clorox bottles strung up there to rattle in the wind and keep the birds and squirrels away from my tomato plants. In the kitchen there are knives in drawers. In the kitchen, there are other possibilities, since I have gone and let her into my house, like she thinks I don't remember that night in Savannah and all those crazy women in their fancy dresses and what they wanted to do to me and how they left me in a room with a talking bear and a boy in a dress who was no boy at all. *And I saw another mighty angel come down from heaven, clothed with a cloud: and a rainbow was upon his head, and his face was as it were the*

*sun, and his feet as pillars of fire: And he had in his hand a little boo,
open: and he set his right foot upon the sea, and his left foot on the earth
And cried with a loud voice, as when a lion roars: and when he had criea
seven thunders uttered their voices.* I almost say that, the Book o
Revelations, Chapter 10, but I don't because Momma always said wha
she said about casting pearls before swine, but just thinking the
thoughts, and walking the halls of my paintings and words with her ir
front of me when she should have been behind me, just all that, anc
just staring at the floor and my dirty bare feet, I'm all the way back a
that night in that Wayne County field not so far away from Savannal
and the house ringed with live oaks and magnolia trees, and the ange
has come down to me because I told it I wanted answers if I was gonna
do what it wanted *this* time. "They're really beautiful," says the woman
who told me her name was Isolde. No, who told me she had *calle*
herself Isolde back then, and maybe she don't think I know the differ
ence. She says "They're really beautiful," as if she means it, but I know
better. I know she looks at them and trembles in her soul, because even
all these years later she is exactly what she was that night, or I'm afraic
she is, and I've let her in my house when I didn't have to. But, anyway
I'm all the way back at that night in the field by the old plantatior
house, and it's after I talked to the gator and the possum, and I've
called down the angel, and it comes all wrapped in fire, just like i
always comes. The sword held above its faces, the sword which I know
is no sword at all, not the way my knife really is a knife. *Then one of th
seraphim flew to me with a burning coal in his hand, which he had taker
from the altar with tongs.* I shield my eyes. I would go blind if I did no
every time shield my eyes, and I say to the angel, "She ain't never killed
anyone. Did you know that? Did you know all she kills is animals anc
not people? Did you know that and not tell me?" The angel howls, anc
I know the words that others might only hear as howling, as the holy
words are only comprehensible words if you are *meant* to know thei
meaning, and this time the meaning is that it shouldn't matter to me

if she only kills beasts, beasts without even souls, that it isn't my place to question and it never has been. This is not long after the house in Savannah and the broken bottle and the gun blowing up in that crazy lady's hands and killing her, all of that, and the fat man with the monsters sleeping in the trunk of his car gave me a ride, *another* ride, only he wasn't going the way he'd said and he left me at a gas station by the Altamaha River. "I think there's something you're meant to do here," he said and then drove off, pretty as you please, and sure as I have let this witch and this cannibal into my house when I didn't have to, sure as that, the angel said yeah, I did have something to do down there, so who was the fat man working for, anyhow? I mean, I *asked* that, but the angel didn't tell me. But this is later on, and I'm telling the angel what the gator and the possum told me about the girl in the river, and the angel gazes down on me in fire and speaks in thunder and swings that sword that is really a burning coal from the altar of Heaven, and the answer is simply, "It doesn't matter. She has to die tonight. She is an abomination in the eyes of your maker." And what I said next, I don't know now even why I said it. I was tired. I was still scared from Savannah when I was not ever in the habit of being scared. But I said, "Then let my *maker* come on down here and kill her, if all she's done is eat animals just like all the rest of us do." And what it showed me then, the whirlwind, the thorn tree, all the rest of it, and how I was not left only a small handful of ashes I do not know, but off I went into that field and I killed her. And I left my knife laying in the dirt and the weeds, and I said that would be the last, that I was done, and the angel touched my forehead and left a mark there, and I don't know if the woman I have let into my house can see it or if she cannot, but it's there, either way and always will be. *Then the Lord put a mark on Cain so that no one who found him would kill him.* Maybe she saw it and just thinks I bumped my head. Maybe she thinks it's a birthmark. But it means she cannot kill me, whatever she intends and whether she has seen it or not seen it, it means that she cannot kill me. She's only a small witch, and she cannot ignore the fingerprints of angels. And that night, when I had done what I was sent into the field that once had been cotton and slaves and mules to do and when there was nothing left of the girl from the river, the angel said I would want for nothing ever again, because I had been a righteous soldier, even if I fell short, even if I stopped before the war was done, my part in the fighting and so on. I would not want. "It really is a lovely house," the woman says, the woman who only called herself Isolde that night in Savannah when she and the others meant to cut my throat and disembowel me and cook me and eat me. I had not even been sent to kill them, though they ate people and desecrated the dead, but I was supposed to murder that sad, pathetic thing in the river, like a panther trapped inside a cage when it was not even really a panther in there at all. And finally, finally, finally we have reached the kitchen, and I offer her a seat at my table, and I offer her coffee or hot tea or a cold drink. She smiles, and I don't like that smile, even if I cannot find anything wrong with it. She says tea, please, and now she's talking about riding a bus, like I have not ever done that in my life, like I need to understand what riding a bus means, and I wish I were back upstairs, wishing she would stop knocking and stop ringing the doorbell and go away. I put water in the tea pot, and I set it on the stove, and I take down a cup from the cabinet. And the kitchen is filled with morning sunlight like fire from the eyes of an angel.

(October 2018)

Years ago, the walls of the kitchen were painted the palest shade of pink, and the countertops are pink Formica that doesn't quite match the walls, and the pink refrigerator doesn't really match either one. The floor is divided up into squares of black and white linoleum, like a chessboard, scuffed and scratched by hundreds of feet, and on the window above the rust-stained sink are chintz curtains, tiny pink

lowers printed on a field of yellow; the curtains badly need to be
aken down and washed. The woman whose name has never been
solde Penderghast sits at the kitchen table and sips her tea, which has
one cold, and Dancy, still wearing her sunglasses, sits across from
er and stares at her hands and the pattern on the pink-and-white
ilcloth and into the murky depths of her own teacup. The cups are
hipped and cracked, bought second-hand from Goodwill or some
ther thrift store, like almost everything else in the house, but they're
ot *so* chipped and cracked that they leak.

Dancy's been talking, and the woman's been listening. She
loesn't interrupt. She waits until she's sure Dancy has finished, that
he's come to the end of the tale of the possum and the alligator and
he girl in the river, before she says anything. And then she asks, "So,
t was over? Just like that, you were done with it, all of it. The angel
ust let you walk away?"

Dancy nods, but she doesn't look up. "Just like that," she says. "I
cilled the girl in the field, and then I walked away. I went where the
ngel said I should go. I came here. It was over, and I came here, to
his place that had been set aside for me."

But it wasn't really over, she thinks. *It won't ever be really over.* But
his isn't anything she feels like trying to explain, not to this woman
nd on this morning and probably not ever.

"It really is a very lovely house," the woman tells her for the fifth
r sixth time since Dancy let her inside. Dancy knows that's only
)ecause the woman's nervous, but she's still tired of hearing it.

"It isn't all that much," she says. "Someplace to stay out of the rain
nd out of the sun and the cold. A place no one can ever make me
eave. But it's only the meanest portion, the tiniest little bit of what
night have been mine, if I hadn't quit. That's what the angel told me
hat night, how a seat had been made for me at the right hand..." but
hen she trails off, because exactly what the angel said she was giving
ıp is just one more thing Dancy doesn't feel like trying to explain.

"That old house in Savannah," the woman says, "I went bac there one night and burned it to the ground."

Dancy glances up at her, just for a moment or two, and then bac down at the table and at her hands and the cup.

"You killed them all?" Dancy asks her. "All the other ones?"

"No," the woman says. "They'd already left the city a long tim before then. Biancabella and Candida went up to Rhode Island Madeline, she went home to New Orleans. Mary Rose didn't say wher she was going, but I got a postcard from her once, from Los Angeles.

"Candida," Dancy says. "Isn't that what you call a yeast infection? She straightens her sunglasses.

"Yeah, well…we used to tease her about that," the woman says "but it's also a name, a Latin name. It means 'dazzling white.' Georg Bernard Shaw wrote a play named 'Candida.'"

Dancy's never heard of anyone named George Bernard Shaw, bu she lets the matter drop. "So, you didn't kill none of them?" she asks

"No, I didn't kill anyone. None of them, I mean. I don't think ever could have."

"But you killed other folks," says Dancy. "You killed other folk and ate them."

"It's complicated," the woman replies.

"No, it ain't," says Dancy. "You just say that so you don't gott think on it too hard."

The pink refrigerator makes a sudden wet chugging sound, bu Dancy ignores it, and it stops a few seconds later.

"I was just a kid," the woman says. "Both of us were just kids."

"And you think that makes a difference?"

"I think it's important to take into account, that's all."

Dancy turns in her seat, and she squints at the kitchen win dow and the dirty chintz curtains, at the late morning light an the dogwood tree outside the window and a stingy patch of blu October sky.

"We both of us done what we done," she says. "Sometimes, I try to convince myself none of it was real, that I was crazy and it wasn't nothin' but the things crazy women see. But there's this house, and there's money every month. Every month I find money in a Ball Mason jar on the back steps, so I can pay the bills and buy food and all. I don't know where else it would come from, except from the angel, or someone works for the angel. And it means no matter how hard I try and make like it didn't happen, I'm just lying to myself, because I'm a sinner in the hands of an angry God, just like every damn body else in this sorry world."

"Well, I'm sorry if my coming here's upset you," the woman says.

"You ain't upset me," says Dancy. "The sorts of things I carry round inside my head and have to dream about and have to remember, next to all *that,* you ain't much of nothin', really. It took me by surprise, is all. Your showin' up like a bolt outta the blue, expectin' whatever it is you're expectin' from me. Absolution? Forgiveness? You gonna tell me now how it wasn't your fault, bein' with all those others? You gonna tell how you was beaten on by your pa or raped by an uncle or how your momma was maybe a drug fiend, so you ran away from home, and them ladies in that house took you in, out of the charitable kindness of their hearts, when no one else would? How *you* done what *they* done so that they'd let you stay or because you felt obligated, and that's the *only* reason?"

The slight, green-eyed woman doesn't answer right away. She takes another sip of her tea, then she looks at the kitchen window, too.

"No," she says. "I won't tell you any of those things, because they aren't the truth. And no, I'm not asking you to forgive me."

"Well, then I guess that's somethin', at least," says Dancy. "You got any place to go? After you leave here, I mean?"

"Not really," the woman replies. "I gave up my apartment in Savannah. I couldn't afford the rent, anyway. I had a job, but...no, not really."

"You got a real name, a Christian name your mother and your father gave you when you was born?"

"Sophia," the woman tells her, "but they always called me Sophie. My parents called me Sophie. It was one of my aunts' names. My mom's sister."

"Sophie," Dancy Flammarion says, half to herself, and then she says it again. It isn't a bad name.

"I thought you might try and kill me, if I came here," says Sophie, and Dancy finally stops squinting at the kitchen window and stares at her, instead.

"But you came anyway," Dancy says, and then she gets up and goes to the pink refrigerator and opens it and takes out a bottle of Buffalo Rock ginger ale, and she holds it against her forehead.

"Yeah, I came anyway."

"What would be the point in killin' you?" Dancy asks, twisting the cap off the bottle, setting the cap on the pink Formica countertop. "Who would even care anymore or even notice? And the way it all was at the end, who's there to say I didn't do just as bad my own self, once or twice?"

"The angel might," says Sophie.

Dancy takes a swallow of the Buffalo Rock, and then she points at the ceiling. "I gotta spare room," she says, "if you need it. If you want it. If you got nowhere else to be."

First I let her in my house, she thinks, *when all I had to do was lay there and wait for her to go away, and now I'm offerin' her shelter under my roof.* And Dancy also thinks, *Maybe that's so I can kill her later on, when I'm ready, like I ought'a killed them all.* But that isn't it, and she knows that isn't it. She wonders if maybe the jars of money will stop showing up on the back-porch steps, and she wonders what she'd do if they did.

"It's very generous of you, but I couldn't do that," says Sophie. "I couldn't impose like that."

"You got nowhere else to be. You said so yourself, so you *can* do t. You can help out. There are things you can do around here. Most lays I don't like goin' out, so you can do the errands."

Dancy hears the bat-winged werewolves upstairs laughing at her, aughing at her fit to beat the band, but she ignores them same as she gnored the old refrigerator.

"I don't know," says Sophie, and Dancy Flammarion says, "Well, hink about it. You got some time, I reckon. You ain't come after no all of fire."

"Sure, I've got some time."

"Then think about it," Dancy says again, and Sophie says she vill, and she also thinks about how the albino woman in her bathrobe and sunglasses looks so much older than she should.

But then so would I, if I'd done half of what she did. If I'd lived through what she must have lived through and seen everything she must have been witness to. If they ever told stories about me like they used to tell about her.

And then the slight, green-eyed woman named Sophie, who was never named Isolde Penderghast and who once lived in a terrible old house in Savannah, she sits at the table watching Dancy, and Dancy stands at the kitchen counter and drinks her ginger ale, and before long the morning has become the afternoon.

With grateful regards to the memory of Walt Kelly.

REQUIEM

I'd sorta *wanted* this to be the very last Dancy story ever, but…well, if you've skipped ahead and read the afterword then you already know that "Refugees" came along about two and half months later and foiled that plan. On the one hand, "Requiem" is a pretty straightforward postscript or footnote or sequel or what-the-hell-ever to "Les Fleurs Empoisonnées." On the other, it's me punching both the Dark Horse *Alabaster* graphic novels and *Threshold* in the face. I needed an ending for Dancy that seemed truer than her end in either of those stories, and this one rings fairly true to me. Of course, it's not the *very* end.

Afterword
(DO NOT READ THIS FIRST)

I've been keeping the company of Dancy Flammarion for a very long time now. No other character of mine has proven so stubbornly durable, and maybe someone will come along someday, with nothing better to do and figure out why. Me, I honestly can't say. Maybe it's because she's being written from my lifelong complicated relationship with the American South. Maybe it's because her roots lie in my own childhood and my enduring love affair with Sergio Leone's "Man With No Name."

Oh, c'mon. Surely you've already noticed the similarity between Dancy Flammarion and Clint Eastwood.

Dancy makes her first appearance in my second novel, *Threshold* (2001), and I honestly thought that's all the need I'd have of her. As I recounted in the preface of *Alabaster* (2006), the earliest mention I can find of her in my notes for that novel are from September 16th, 1998. That means she's been with me, in one form or another, for twenty-one years! Anyway, in the preface to that collection I recount how she's named for both Dancy, Alabama and the astronomer Nicolas Camille Flammarion (1842–1925) and how, shortly after having finished *Threshold* in May of 2000, I discovered that I wanted to continue writing stories about Dancy Flammarion. Sure, she'd died in the book, but there was the question of what she'd been up to before appearing in Birmingham, the misadventures briefly alluded to at the end of Chapter Eight.

So, in June and July of 2001 I wrote "In the Garden of Poisonous Flowers" (*id est* "Les Fleurs Empoisonnées"), set only a few weeks before the beginning of *Threshold,* and then, at the end of October 2001, I wrote "The Well of Stars and Shadow," my second Dancy story…and after that they just sorta kept on coming, until there were enough that Subterranean Press could compile them into a collection, *Alabaster.*

And I honestly, truly, thought that was the end of it.

And, indeed, I didn't come back to Dancy again for several years, not until the autumn of 2010. While in Portland, Oregon for the H.P. Lovecraft Film Festival, I had a meeting with an editor from Dark Horse Comics. They wanted to work with me, she said. I was reluctant to get involved in comics again, I said, after the mess that had been my time at DC/Vertigo, back in the 1990s. Fine, said the editor, then just write us a prose story for *Dark Horse Presents.* I agreed, and in November we decided it would be a Dancy story, and we also agreed to ask Ted Naifeh, who'd illustrated *Alabaster,* to illustrate the story. So, a little later, between the 7th and 9th of April 2011, I wrote a fairly short tale, "Bus Fare," in which Dancy meets a talkative bird and a sexy werewolf named Maisie Satterfield.

There, I thought – for the third time – *I'm done with Dancy Flammarion. There are no more stories about her left to tell.*

But I was very wrong.

I often am.

In June, three months after I finished "Bus Fare," I got the news that Dark Horse founder Mike Richardson wanted to see the story expanded into a graphic novel mini-series. And even though I'd said I never, ever wanted to work in comics again (and thought that I'd meant it), I pitched *Alabaster: Wolves* as a five-issue series. They liked it. Steve Lieber was hired to draw the book, with Rachelle Rosenberg handling the colors and Greg Ruth painting the covers. Suddenly, everyone was excited. I was told this was going to be big. I was told this was going to be *really* big. The *Buffy the Vampire Slayer* comic was ending and Dark Horse was looking at Dancy Flammarion as "the next Buffy Summers." I was told that, after the mini-series, *Alabaster* would be that holiest grail of the comic industry – *a monthly title.*

My agent got happy. I got happy. Film and merchandising rights were haggled over. I was sworn to secrecy. It was a very weird and giddy time, and I had no idea that it was actually the beginning of a long nightmare. Rather, I thought that, finally, it was the beginning of mainstream success and the financial security it brings.

Yeah, well. Anyway...

That's what *didn't* happen.

Sure, maybe in some alternate reality it all worked out swell, and there was even a feature film, with Elle Fanning as Dancy and Sid Haig as the Bailiff and Anne Hathaway as the matriarch of the Stephens Ward Tea League and Society of Resurrectionists. That's a happy thought.

But in *this* worldline, Steve and Rachelle and Greg and I produced a kickass book, and in the winter of 2011–2012 I did about a billion interviews, and Dark Horse put a big marketing push behind *Alabaster: Wolves* and absolutely every industry publication adored it. The glowing reviews poured in. I was told that a monthly series would be officially green-lit in late February. Then I was told, no, I'd get the go-ahead by the middle of March. But no go-ahead arrived, and weird shit started to happen. You know, storm clouds suddenly appearing on the horizon and so on and so forth. My editor wouldn't give me a definite answer because Mike Richardson wouldn't give *her* a definite answer because, supposedly, the committee that held the purse strings wouldn't give *him* a definite answer. And then on March

21st I got the bad news. Despite all the great reviews and good pre-orders for the first issue and also despite everything I'd been assured since the previous summer, we were gonna have to wait and see if the sales of the first mini-series were sufficient to warrant a monthly. That was one of those black days that make me wanna pack it in forever and never write another fucking word.

It was *that* bad.

I should have walked away from Dark Horse then and there, but I didn't. Hope springs eternal, and hope is a stone-cold bitch.

I was told we had to make sure those sales figures were not merely good, but stellar, and that there would be a hardback collecting the mini, and in the meantime we'd keep the title on life support with monthly installments in *Dark Horse Presents.* Thirteen of those were planned and produced, at eight pages each, and Steve and Rachelle and Greg stayed onboard. But those crucial sales were *not* stellar. Sales were just okay, and just okay is never good enough.

In February 2013, the *Alabaster: Wolves* hardback was released (and, ironically, that summer it would garner me my second Bram Stoker Award). That same month, my editor at Dark Horse left and I got a new editor. The *Dark Horse Presents* installments continued through-out that year – giving me small but regular checks – printed under the title *Alabaster: Boxcar Tales,* the last of which appeared in *DHP* #32 (January 2014 cover date). They were collected, in May 2014, as *Alabaster: Grimmer Tales.* I doubt it sold very well, but I honestly never bothered to find out.

At least, I thought, the fiasco was over and done with.

I tried to put Dark Horse behind me. I tried hard.

This was not to be. Not yet.

In the autumn of 2013, my editor informed me I could do a second mini-series, if I wanted (I suppose I have the Stoker to thank for this). I needed the money, so I said yes – even though I'd killed Dancy off – once again – at the end of *Grimmer Tales.*

See, that's how this fuckery keeps happening to me, because I always, always, *always* need the money. Over the next year and several months I would write *Alabaster: The Good, the Bad, and the Bird* (Hey, kids, look! There's Sergio Leone and Clint Eastwood again!), and that ill-advised endeavor would be, let's not mince words, a *shitstorm,* in every way that doing a comic can *be* a shitstorm. You know in *Apocalypse Now* where Martin Sheen says that bit about wanting a mission and "for my sins they gave me one"? Well, let me tell you, Colonel Walter E. Kurtz had nothing on the writing and production of *Alabaster: The Good, the Bad, and the Bird.* To start with, we were going with a different artist than Steve Lieber. I was promised Joe Querio, whose work I fucking adore. Well, that didn't work out. No idea why. I've forgotten. Other names were floated about, but eventually, finally, we landed Joelle Jones, whose work I also adore and who could draw Dancy like nobody's business.

Even so, from the very beginning, my heart was not in this book, not after all the crap I'd already endured at the hands of Dark Horse. My deadline for the first script was May 14th, and I blew that *by months.* I kept starting and stopping and changing the storyline and setting the book aside to work on other things. Frankly, I had zero enthusiasm for the project, and I just kept losing interest. Plus, 2014 was the year I turned fifty, which did nothing pleasant for my state of mind.

Finally, in January 2015, I retreated to a cabin in the Catskills (thank you, Neil), because I figured if I was snowed in, I'd finally *have* to finish the thing. And I was. And I did. But then, BOOM, in mid-February (I was still in that cabin in the Catskills), Joelle Jones quit, because her mini-series *Lady Killer* had done well and Dark Horse wanted to make it a monthly (they never did), and my editor wanted to know would I please help them choose another artist? I said no. In fact, I said, "You know what? I quit. Here's the scripts, do whatever you want with them. I've been paid, and the checks didn't bounce, so I no longer care. I no longer want to be involved. I need to write a novel."

Well, I said something like that.

Mike Richardson called my agent in NYC to talk her into trying to talk me into *un*quitting. No, really. That actually happened.

I'm leaving out all sorts of stuff that makes this sad, sordid mess even more sad and sordid, but recounting my time at Dark Horse is really beginning to piss me off all over again. Some wounds fester pretty much forever, at least if you're me. So, let's hurry and wrap this up, please.

I unquit, and *Alabaster: The Good, the Bad, and the Bird* got a new artist, someone with whom I was never happy, someone who drew mountains in Selma, Alabama, where there are no mountains, and Rachelle Rosenberg had left for greener pastures (and who could blame her), but at least we still had gorgeous covers by Greg Ruth. The series was released the next year, then collected as a hardback late in the summer of 2016, and that was that, once and for all.

Finally.

There, said the weary writer, *I promise, I am done with you, Dancy. You've been through enough. You've been through King Nebuchadnezzar's goddamn fiery furnace. Sorry it didn't work out, kid. Have a good life. Or afterlife. Or whatever.*

This turned out to be a promise that I was either unable or unwilling to keep. Or maybe it was a promise I should never have made. Regardless, on April 17th, 2015, before the dust from that long nightmare had even settled, I began a new Dancy short story, "Dancy vs. the Pterosaur." One morning in Providence, I found myself wanting to reclaim the character, to jettison Bird and Maisie (well, mostly) and all the silly, convoluted, dot-to-dot-to-dot story-arc plotting that had marred the comics. I wanted to *take her back,* as they say. "Dancy vs. the Pterosaur" appeared that same month in *Sirenia Digest* No. 111. And then, in January and February of 2017, less than a year later, I wrote a much longer (and weirder) Dancy tale, "Tupelo (1998)." I really liked these two new stories. They felt nothing at all like the comics, even if they also didn't feel the same as the stories in *Alabaster*. Anyway, eleven or so months after finishing "Tupelo (1998)" I found myself needing a chapbook to accompany the forthcoming collection *The Dinosaur Tourist* (Subterranean Press, 2018), and I suggested to Bill Schafer that it could be the three uncollected Dancy Flammarion stories (including the original prose version of "Bus Fare").

That was the plan for a time, but then, on February 9, 2018, I told Bill that looking over the proposed three-story Dancy chapbook, which came to over thirty-one thousand words, it seemed a shame not to add another story or two and publish a full-fledged second Dancy short-story collection. He agreed, and I promised him the new material by year's end. However, that spring we left Providence and moved back to Birmingham – and there were many other inconvenient things – and, surprise, I blew the deadline (by a year) and didn't actually get around to writing the two new Dancy stories, "Dreams of a Poor Wayfaring Stranger" and "Requiem," until May and June of 2019. The collection should have been complete at that point, only we still needed the customary bonus chapbook, which led me, this past October, to write *just one more* Dancy tale, "Refugees."

Which brings us to *now*.

And *now* there's one last thing, a final, niggling detail, and then I'll shut up and you can read the book proper – the problem of continuity between and within the Dancy stories. I imagine even the laziest, least attentive reader will realize that all this stuff does not add up to some sort of coherent, internally-consistent narrative whole. Not even close. In truth, there are, by my reckoning, a minimum of four distinct Dancy continuities, which, if you care to break it all down, look something like this:

1. Dancy Prime: The *Threshold* storyline. Dancy arrives in Birmingham after all that weird shit in Florida (and weird shit elsewhere that's only hinted at) and dies outside the gates of the

Birmingham Water Works tunnel. Only not really, because I had to go and write an epilogue the novel would have been better off without.

2. The *Alabaster* Dancy: Theoretically, all those short stories in *Alabaster* should comprise to a tidy "prequel" to *Threshold*. In practice, it really doesn't work. At least, it doesn't work for me, and I should know. By the end of "Les Fleur Empoisonnées, when the Bailiff gives Dancy a ride as far as Macon, things have started to diverge from the *Threshold* timeline. Oh, and forget all that nonsense in the original "Bainbridge" text that tied Dancy to the events of *Silk* and *Murder of Angels*. At best, that was a bad idea. At worst, it was an idiotic idea. In all reprints of the story, those sections have been viciously, ruthlessly excised.

3. The Dark Horse Dancy: There's no way to square this stuff with either *Threshold* or the prose *Alabaster* stories. I pretty much hit reset for the comic. The whole thing starts off with an older Dancy, for example, because there was concern she was too young for a comics heroine. So, instead of fifteen going on sixteen, she's more like nineteen. And in the first two continuities, she never goes to South Carolina, and…et cetera. But like the Dancy Prime continuity, she dies in this one. But then she's resurrected. Well, not really.

4. *Comes a Pale Rider* Dancy: I will freely admit that this one is sort of a wastebasket, and there are probably inconsistencies in the stories I wrote between April 2016 and this past October that would necessitate further nitpicking and hair splitting. But we'll ignore all that bushwa. The new stories ditch the comics continuity and *sorta* circle back around to the prose *Alabaster* continuity, but *only* sorta. For example, "Tupelo (1998)" fits in right before "Highway 97" and "Bainbridge," and "Requiem" could be read as a loose sequel to "Les Fleur Empoisonnées." But then there's "Dreams of a Poor Wayfaring Stranger," which pretty much gives the very idea of continuity the middle finger. And, to make matters still more confusing, it includes "Bus Fare," which is, of course, actually where the whole mess with

Dark Horse began. Indeed, here and there you will find allusions to both Bird and Maisie, hinting that possibly the Dancy of these stories exists in a universe just next door to the Dancy of the comics and that the walls of those two universes are kind of leaky. Indeed, in "Refugees" Dancy encounters a dead red-wing blackbird who's pretty much Bird's doppelgänger. And note that in *Comes a Pale Horse*, Dancy is permitted to grow old, rather than die as a teenager. When all's said and done, I'd say that this fourth continuity is at best a *anti-continuity*. And look at me inventing obnoxious, newfangledly words like some kind of damned annoying literary theorist or sociologist or third-wave feminist critic or what have you.

So, there you go. Questions answered, even if they were never actually asked, because I'm pedantic, and you're welcome. And as to whether the tales in *Comes a Pale Rider* (and the accompanying chap-book) are the concluding episodes of Dancy Flammarion's story and I've finally, *finally*, for really and truly, gotten her out of my system, or if there will inevitably, sooner or later, be more, well…what the fuck d'you think?

Caitlín R. Kiernan
7 November 2019
Birmingham, Alabama

Copyright Information

Author's Biography

Caitlín R. Kiernan is the author of thirteen novels, including *The Drowning Girl: A Memoir,* recipient of the Bram Stoker and James Tiptree, Jr. awards, and a nominee for the Locus Award, Nebula Award, Shirley Jackson Award, Mythopoeic Fantasy Award for Adult Literature, British Fantasy Award, and World Fantasy Award. A prolific short-fiction author, their stories have previously been collected in *Tales of Pain and Wonder* (2000), *Wrong Things* (2001, with Poppy Z. Brite), *From Weird and Distant Shores* (2002), *To Charles Fort, With Love* (2005), *Alabaster* (2006), *A is for Alien* (2009), *The Ammonite Violin & Others* (2010), *Confessions of a Five-Chambered Heart* (2012), the World Fantasy Award-winning *The Ape's Wife and Other Tales* (2013), *Dear Sweet Filthy World* (2017), *Houses Under the Sea* (2018), and *The Dinosaur Tourist* (2018), as well as two volumes of "weird erotica," *Frog Toes and Tentacles* (2005) and *Tales from the Woeful Platypus* (2007). Subterranean Press has released a two-volume set collecting the best of Kiernan's short fiction, *Two Worlds and In Between* (2011) and *Beneath an Oil-Dark Sea* (2015), and in 2019 Tachyon Publications released *The Very Best of Caitlín R. Kiernan.* Their "The Prayer of Ninety Cats" received a 2014 World Fantasy Award. Recently, Tor.com has published their trilogy of Lovecraftian espionage novellas, *Agents of Dreamland* (2017), *Black Helicopters* (2018), and *The Tindalos Asset* (2020) known collectively. Kiernan worked with DC/Vertigo on *The Dreaming* (1996–2000), as well as *The Girl Who Would Be Death* (1998–1999) and *Bast: Eternity Game* (2002). In 2011, they returned to comics with the Bram Stoker Award-winning *Alabaster: Wolves* (Dark Horse, 2012), followed by *Alabaster: Grimmer Tales* (2012–2014) and *Alabaster: The Good, the Bad, and the Bird* (2015–2016). Kiernan is also a vertebrate paleontologist and is currently a fossil preparator and research associate at the McWane Science Center in Birmingham, Alabama. Recently, they coathored *"Asmodochelys parhami,* a new fossil marine turtle from the Campanian Demopolis Chalk and the stratigraphic congruence of competing marine turtle phylogenies," based in part on a specimen they discovered in 2001. Currently, they live in Mountain Brook, Alabama with their partner Kathryn and their two cats, Selwyn and Lydia.